THE APPROACHING STORM

LARRY NABBS

Read With You Publishing

Text copyright © 2016 Larry Nabbs

Published by Read With You Publishing

ISBN-13: 978-1-944710-08-8
ISBN-10: 1-944710-08-6

Printed in the United States of America

Contents

CHAPTER 1 1
CHAPTER 2 4
CHAPTER 3 6
CHAPTER 4 10
CHAPTER 5 15
CHAPTER 6 19
CHAPTER 7 22
CHAPTER 8 26
CHAPTER 9 32
CHAPTER 10 38
CHAPTER 11 44
CHAPTER 12 50
CHAPTER 13 53
CHAPTER 14 60
CHAPTER 15 69
CHAPTER 16 74
CHAPTER 17 77
CHAPTER 18 82
CHAPTER 19 93
CHAPTER 20 96
CHAPTER 21 103
CHAPTER 22 110
CHAPTER 23 114
CHAPTER 24 121
CHAPTER 25 131

CHAPTER 26..139
CHAPTER 27..149
CHAPTER 28..154
CHAPTER 29..159
CHAPTER 30..166
CHAPTER 31..171
CHAPTER 32..176
CHAPTER 33..182
CHAPTER 34..191
CHAPTER 35..196
CHAPTER 36..201
CHAPTER 37..205
CHAPTER 38..218
CHAPTER 39..225
CHAPTER 40..235
CHAPTER 41..241

CHAPTER 1

Nothing happened.

Nothing ever happened.

At least, that's what Jimmy thought as he stared out of his bedroom window. Mind you, it 'was' Four o'clock in the morning, and everybody else was probably sleeping, but he couldn't sleep. Jimmy was a ten-year old child, an orphan, and this was his fourth foster home in two months. He was restless, he was always restless, anticipating that something bad would happen, as it always did. Maybe it was because he 'thought' something bad would happen that it happened. Maybe if he stopped thinking about bad things that could happen, they wouldn't happen, or maybe it was just that he was unlucky with his foster parents, either that, or they were unlucky with him. He was quiet, everybody said that he was quiet, too quiet. The second foster parents complained, "We don't what he's thinking." Possibly, he wasn't thinking anything, nothing at all, he was just busy 'being'. He tried to fit in, tried to smile, but there was always something false in his smile, as if he were not trying hard enough. But he did try. He couldn't help being sad, and he couldn't help being quiet, it was who he was. Unfortunately, nobody ever really accepted who he was, they wanted to change him, they wanted him to be someone he wasn't, someone who 'they' wanted him to be, and he couldn't, try as he might, he couldn't, and so, once again, Jimmy sat up gazing out of the bedroom window at Four o'clock in the morning.

The street outside was quiet, deathly quiet.

Not a dog barked, not a cat meowed, not one leaf stirred in the stillness of the night.

Jimmy felt lonely.

It wouldn't have mattered if he'd been surrounded by crowds of people, he would have still felt lonely. But here, in the darkness of his bedroom and the night outside, his feeling of loneliness was magnified, more poignant, like a single candle, flickering amidst a huge ocean of dark dreams.

It was as he was having these thoughts, thoughts he usually had on nights such as this, that he saw a dark shape casting a long shadow beneath the light of a streetlamp. Jimmy stared at it, his eyes widening as he did so. It wasn't a cat or a dog, nor a person, it was something relatively human-shaped, and yet somehow, not human.

Jimmy watched as the dark figure crept, as if it were hunting something in the night. Jimmy leaned forward onto the window sill peering across the darkened street, trying to see the figure clearly through the window. Suddenly, the figure stopped, and then its head turned slowly. Jimmy could now make out the grotesque features of its face. It looked like a monster, just like something from a nightmare, something for small children and even adults to be afraid of. Now, Jimmy could see its eyes. They were blazing red, as if they were burning with a fire inside them.

The grotesque figure raised its head, and then its eyes met Jimmy's and stared directly at him, its eyes burning directly into his with a fierce red glowing light. Jimmy gasped and pushed himself back from the window, falling to the floor. As he sat on the floor breathing heavily, he heard a noise outside in the darkness. It was like a howl, a creepy animal-like howl that sent shivers down Jimmy's spine. Jimmy remained on the floor, staring up at the window and unable to move.

And then, there was silence.

Jimmy waited for a moment, then crept slowly back up to the window and once again peeped outside.

The dark shape was now gone.

The streetlamp shone dimly onto the road below. The street was once again deserted, quiet. That night, Jimmy didn't sleep, he remained wide awake staring down at the street beneath his window. He finally fell asleep just as the sun was rising and beginning to fill his bedroom with early morning light. Jimmy slept with his head on the window sill as the street below slowly came to life.

CHAPTER 2

"But I saw it!" Jimmy said to his new foster mother, Mrs. Bennet, as she was preparing his breakfast.

"You saw nothing!" Mrs. Bennet said, busy at the stove.

She was a strict woman in her forties with an imposing figure.

"It was just a nightmare! That's all! If you slept normal hours like everyone else you wouldn't be seeing things or having nightmares at all! The orphanage warned us about you! They told us about your tall stories! Apparently, that's the only time you talk, isn't it? To tell tales! Well, you'll have to shake yourself out of it my boy! You'll never get through life like that! It's no wonder you never make any friends! But don't worry! Me and my husband, Albert, we'll shake you out of it! You mark my words! A few months with us and ... "

But as Mrs. Bennet rattled on and on, Jimmy sat with his head down, closing his eyes and placing his hands over his ears. He'd heard it all before. Each foster parent lectured him, telling him that he must change, and telling him how they would change him.

Jimmy went to school that morning feeling depressed. It was another new school, another place where it was difficult for him to make new friends. There were bullies as usual, and as usual they picked on him, bullying him everyday. The teacher, Miss Strong, asked the class to write an essay on happiness. The other children immediately began to write things down, but not Jimmy. He sat in front of a blank sheet of paper with his pencil ready to write, but he had no thoughts, absolutely no ideas at all on the subject of happiness. That morning, Miss Strong took him to the headmaster, Mr. Ork, a huge imposing man, and told him that Jimmy refused to work. Jimmy was punished. The headmaster caned each of his hands and his backside twice. Tears came to Jimmy's eyes, although, he was not crying. Later, during the break for lunch, it was time for the bullies to start on him again. When school finished, Jimmy went home dragging his feet. Happiness? he thought. What is happiness? And try as he might, he could find no answer to that question. No answer at all.

That night, he ran away. He ran away as far as he could.

CHAPTER 3

The 'lost people' slept under bridges, in parks, in street doorways, sleeping wherever they could. Some people called them tramps, others called them the road people, but they preferred the name, 'lost people'. In fact, they were not really lost, they knew exactly 'where' they were, but they thought the name sounded better, much better than 'tramps' anyway, and in some ways, they 'were' a little lost, in their minds. The lost people didn't have much to eat, didn't have much of anything, but they took Jimmy in and helped him, sharing with him what little they had. Sometimes there were fights, sometimes those who liked to drink would go crazy, shouting and hitting anyone. At first, it was hard, but Jimmy learned to avoid the trouble with the help of one woman, a Mrs. Tingle. She took a shine to Jimmy and protected him. From time to time, the police made their rounds and Jimmy would hide. There were other children too, some younger, some older. Here, life was simple. Survive, survive each day. Jimmy sometimes thought about the subject that the teacher, Miss Strong, had given him to write about. He thought about it often, but never really found an answer. Happiness? Was it a day when you were not beaten? A day when you were not bullied? A day when nobody was shouting at you? Trying to change who you were? A day when you were not cold, freezing cold as you tried to sleep outside in the winter's snow and ice? Was it a day when you were not starving from hunger after having found only some scraps of leftovers to eat? Or was it a day when you had somewhere safe to sleep? Maybe it was all of these things together. Jimmy had had days like this, but the word 'happiness' seemed to be a 'magical' word somehow, a word filled with feelings, feelings he did not know, feelings that were continually out of his reach.

*

Not knowing where else to go, Jimmy grew up living with the 'lost people'. He was now seventeen years old. He had learned how to fend for himself, how to survive, and how to hide when necessary. Since that night in the bedroom, when he had gazed out of the window and had seen the strange grotesque creature in the shadows, he had been afraid of the darkness and had always slept nearby the lost people's fire, or sometimes, when there was no fire, nearby a light of some kind.

The image of the creature that night had been imprinted upon his mind, and it was something that he could not forget.

*

It was a bright sunny morning when he saw her. She looked as pretty and as fresh as a Spring flower. Jimmy had been sorting through a bin full of rubbish, looking for any scraps of food that people might have thrown away, when he heard her laughter. She must have been about nineteen years old, and she was wearing a bright pink blouse and a tartan plaid skirt. Her long golden hair shone in the sunlight and her eyes sparkled as she laughed. She was with two other girls, one of whom was quite tall with long brown hair, and the other was of medium-height with shoulder-length black hair. Although each of the other two girls were also very pretty, it was the girl with the golden hair that Jimmy was attracted to. There was something about her, something ... untouchable. It was as if she lived on another planet, in another world. Jimmy closed the bin staring across the street at the three girls as they walked. The more they walked away from him, the more he wanted to see them, to listen to them, to hear the sound of their carefree laughter, and so he began to follow them. He had no thoughts of doing anything to hurt them or disturb them, he merely wanted to be close to them, close to their world, and especially close to the girl with the golden hair. He followed them as they walked to the end of the street, and then they turned right. Jimmy ran along the street and reached the corner where they had turned. He stopped, hesitating, then glanced around the corner. He watched as the girls walked across the street towards a modern residential tower. As the girls approached the building, one of them glanced back and noticed him. It was the girl with the black shoulder-length hair. She seemed to pause, then said something to the other two girls who were about to enter the tower. As the other girls entered the building, the girl with the black shoulder-length hair turned back and crossed the street towards the corner where Jimmy was standing. Jimmy didn't know what to do, he glanced down, embarrassed as he felt the dark haired girl staring at him as she approached. Jimmy thought of turning to run, but something made him stay. He could hear the girl's footsteps now just a few yards away and getting closer.

A sudden panic went through him and he turned to go.

"Hey, you!" the girl with the black hair shouted to him.

Jimmy stopped, facing away from her but still gazing down at the ground. He remained still as the girl walked up to him and listened as she walked round to stand in front of him.

"Were you following us?" the girl asked.

Jimmy didn't look up, he remained staring down at the ground.

"I ... I ... I ..." he stammered.

The girl studied his dirty and ragged clothes. He was young, possibly nineteen years old the same as her, but obviously a tramp, she thought.

"What is it you want?" she asked. "Money? Food?"

Jimmy seemed frozen to the spot. He wasn't used to anyone talking to him, apart from the lost people, and they didn't usually ask questions.

"Are you ... are you all right?" the girl asked. "Do you ... need any help?"

Suddenly, Jimmy shook his head.

"N ... n ... no!" he blurted out. "I ... I ... I go!" he said hurriedly.

Then he began to walk quickly past her. He could feel her watching him as he went, could feel her eyes on his back. He quickly crossed the street and turned a corner. As soon as he had turned the corner, he stopped, closed his eyes and breathed a sigh of relief. He shouldn't have followed them, he thought. He should have left them alone, left them to their world. Never mingle, the lost people had taught him. You don't fit in ... you don't fit in!

CHAPTER 4

Jimmy sat on a bench in the park.

He was staring towards a fence just beyond the trees. On the other side of the fence was a graveyard. The graveyard always seemed so peaceful, at least, during the daytime. He had never been there at night, he had always been afraid to go there at night. Nobody sat nearby him, nobody ever sat nearby him. People seemed to avoid him. Probably because of his dirty and ragged clothes, he thought, and his long, yellow, unwashed and uncut hair. He tried to wash himself when he could, tried to stay clean, but it wasn't always so easy. He came to the park sometimes to feel peaceful. The park was like a paradise with its flowers, grass and trees, the one place where he could escape the city streets with all its concrete.

As he glanced to the left, he saw them, the three girls he had followed one week earlier. Jimmy quickly glanced down, afraid that the black-haired girl would remember him and try to speak to him again. If she did, he didn't know what to say, he would panic again, be awkward, feel stupid. He hoped that they would walk on by. He closed his eyes, hoping, hoping, hoping ...

He heard their footsteps, heard their laughter, and just as their footsteps neared him, they stopped. He heard them talking and sat still for a moment, listening with his eyes tightly shut. After a few minutes, he slowly began to open them and saw that someone was standing in front of him. He looked up and saw the black-haired girl standing there and staring down at him.

"We meet again," she said.

Jimmy stared up at her, his mouth opening in surprise. He glanced past her and saw her two friends sitting on the bench opposite. The girl with the golden hair looked prettier than ever.

"Don't you ever speak?" the black-haired girl asked, staring down at him.

"I ... I ... I ... " Jimmy stammered, just as he had before.

"My name's Rebecca," the girl said.

She bent down, leaning towards him, "What's your name?" she asked.

Jimmy merely stared up at her. It was as if he was unable to speak.

"You 'do' have a name, right?" Rebecca asked.

Jimmy swallowed hard looking up at her, then he nodded.

"J ... J ... Jimmy," he managed to say.

Rebecca smiled, "Jimmy? That's nice. Where do you live Jimmy?"

Jimmy glanced down, he shook his head.

"You ... don't live anywhere?" Rebecca asked.

"Hey! Rebecca! What are you doing?" the brown-haired girl called over from the opposite bench.

"Yeah!" the golden-haired girl said. "Don't waste your time with someone like that! I mean ... just look at him! I can smell him from here!"

Jimmy stared across at her, his mouth opening in a mixture of surprise and shock at what the golden-haired girl had just said.

"Hey, Rebecca, leave him alone," the brown-haired said. "Can't you see he's just a tramp?"

"And a real dirty one too!" the golden-haired girl added, placing her fingers over her nose to emphasize her point.

Rebecca turned to them.

"Hey, stop being so bad! He might need some help!"

"Help? Look, you can't help every tramp you see!" the golden-haired girl said. "Let him crawl back into the bins where he belongs!"

Rebecca stared back at her two friends, "How can you be so   heartless?" she said.

"Come on!" the golden-haired girl said, turning to her tall brown-haired friend, "Let's go!"

The tall girl nodded and stood up.

The golden-haired girl looked at Rebecca, "If you want to save the world, go ahead! We'll see you back at the club!"

Rebecca watched them walk away.

Jimmy, who was staring at the golden-haired girl as she left, felt as if he'd just been hit by someone wielding a baseball bat.

He watched her go, realizing now more than ever, that she really did live in a different world from his. There are two worlds, Jimmy thought, theirs, and his, two worlds so far apart that nothing could bridge the gap.

Rebecca turned and looked back down at him.

She smiled.

Jimmy looked back up at her and saw her smile. Her smile surprised him, nobody ever smiled at him. The black-haired girl's smile touched him, moved him in a way that he could not put into words. He tried to remember the last time that somebody had smiled at him and couldn't.

"I want you to meet someone," Rebecca said. "They'll give you food, a place to sleep."

Jimmy continued to stare up at her, remaining still.

"You ... do want something to eat, right?" she asked.

So many thoughts went through Jimmy's mind at once. Why was she trying to help him? Who was she? Who did she want him to meet? Where did she want to take him?

Don't mingle! ... Don't mingle! The lost peoples' rule came back to him. He thought about it for a moment, and then it seemed as if his stomach was doing the thinking for him. He was hungry, terribly, terribly hungry. Finally, he nodded, looking up into the girl's kind eyes. Rebecca smiled again, "Okay, let's go!" she said.

Jimmy stood up from the bench staring at her strangely, and then began to follow her along the path towards the park's exit.

CHAPTER 5

The building that Rebecca led Jimmy to was just opposite the park. It was a large old red building, at least one hundred years old. The stonework outside it, although red, was dark, miserable looking, but once inside, Jimmy saw a difference. The building had been decorated, painted to make it look fresh and nice. Rebecca took Jimmy along a corridor on the ground floor and knocked on a bright green door. The door creaked open and a tall man with a beard and glasses looked out.

"Rebecca!" he said with a smile. "Good to see you again!"

He opened the door wider.

Rebecca gestured to Jimmy who was standing timidly behind her.

"Dr. Schultz, this is Jimmy. I think he needs help."

Dr. Schultz looked at Jimmy. He studied him, looking up and down at Jimmy's ragged appearance.

"Yes, I see," he said thoughtfully.

Rebecca glanced at Jimmy, "Dr. Schultz runs a home to look after 'stragglers', people who are 'lost' in society. He'll look after you."

"Yes, yes, of course I will!" Dr. Schultz said, ushering them both into his office. "Please, please, come in!"

Jimmy looked around the office as he entered. The doctor's diplomas hung on the walls, and there were photographs, photographs of the doctor himself with other people, some of them older and some of them younger. Dr. Schultz walked to his desk and pushed a button on the intercom.

"Miss Wong, would you come to my office please? We have a new arrival."

He looked at Rebecca and smiled.

"So, how are things with you Rebecca?"

"Fine," Rebecca said. "I miss doing the voluntary work I did here."

"Well, we'd be happy to have you come back."

Rebecca shrugged, "I wish I could. I worked here for my school project, but now I've got lots of studies, and the exams are coming up."

"Well, when you have more time we'd be pleased to have you."

"Thank you," Rebecca said.

Dr. Schultz looked at Jimmy who was walking around the room and studying the photographs on the walls.

"Where did you find Jimmy?" he asked.

"Oh, you know, in the street, in the park. I've seen him around," Rebecca answered.

The door opened and Miss Wong, an oriental woman in her late twenties, entered wearing a white coat as if she were a doctor in a hospital.

"Miss Wong," Dr. Schultz said, "Could you see to our friend Jimmy here?"

Miss Wong looked at Jimmy.

"He needs a bath, a change of clothes, and of course something to eat," Dr. Schultz said.

Miss Wong, whose face remained expressionless, nodded, "Of course doctor!" she said.

She studied Jimmy, then gestured towards the open door for him to leave, "Come with me!" she said, with a tone of voice that seemed to be an order rather than a request.

Jimmy looked at her as if he were afraid of her, then turned to look at Rebecca with a worried expression.

"It's okay," Rebecca said. "Miss Wong will look after you."

Jimmy hesitated, then thought about the promise of food and slowly moved towards the door.

"When you're ready," Dr. Schultz said to him, "I'll come see you and we can have a little chat."

Jimmy glanced back at him, then turned and left the room, followed by Miss Wong.

"He's not very talkative I'm afraid," Rebecca said. "He seems ... shy, or afraid."

Dr. Schultz nodded, "I've dealt with cases like this before," he said. "Just leave him with us, we'll take care of him."

Rebecca nodded with a smile, "I'm sure you will," she said. "Thank you doctor."

Dr. Schultz shook her hand, "No, thank 'you' Rebecca!" he said, with a smile.

Rebecca said goodbye and left.

Dr. Schultz turned to the photographs on the walls of his office.

"Yes ..." he said softly to himself, his smile now disappearing, as he studied the photographs. "Thank you ... very much!" he said, his voice now sounding cold as he spoke.

CHAPTER 6

Jimmy hated the bath, he thought it was too hot. He also felt embarrassed at being seen naked by Miss Wong. Miss Wong called for another worker, a male worker called Tony, to help with Jimmy's bath. Tony was also in his twenties. He was big and muscular and he held Jimmy still as Miss Wong bathed him. She used a scrubbing brush which felt as if it had nails in it as she scrubbed at Jimmy's body with it. Jimmy tried to resist, splashing in the water and crying out but Tony held him firmly in place. Finally, when his bath was finished, Miss Wong gave him clean clothes to put on. The clothes were a little big for him but they were okay. Jimmy was now dressed completely in white. He was wearing white jean-like trousers, a white sweat shirt and white socks. Only the trainers, which he was given to wear, were not completely white, but were white and black. Miss Wong then went at him with a large pair of scissors to cut away his long hair. She cut his hair down to shoulder length and meant to cut it shorter, but Jimmy put up such a fight that she decided that at least his, now shoulder-length, hair looked a lot neater than before. After that, he was taken to the kitchen and given some food and something to drink. By that time Jimmy was beginning to wonder if it was all worth it, but when he tucked into the food, he dismissed all other thoughts and ate as if he hadn't eaten for months. Both Miss Wong and Tony watched him, standing by, waiting until he was finished and could not eat or drink anymore. After, he was taken to a room on the third floor. The room was small but clean and comfortable. Its walls and ceiling were white and smelled like a room in a hospital. There was a single bed, a chair, a chest of drawers and a cupboard. Miss Wong left Jimmy alone and told him that Dr. Schultz would be along later to speak to him and that he should get some rest. When Miss Wong left, Jimmy tried the bed. It was a little hard, but a lot softer than what he was used to. He stood up and looked around the room. Both the chest of drawers and the cupboard were empty. There was a mirror over the chest of drawers and Jimmy caught sight of his reflection in it. He stopped still in his tracks and gazed at himself. It had been so long since he had seen an image of himself in the mirror that he'd almost forgotten what he looked like. What he saw in his reflection startled him. He now moved nearer to the mirror, studying himself closely. He gazed at his reflection with a surprised look on his face. In the mirror, he saw someone new, someone different, someone young and clean, dressed in clean clothes. It was like looking at someone completely different, as if it were a complete stranger who was staring back at him. His eyes were blue, his hair, which was now clean and tidy, was blonde, and although it had been cut, it still hung down in the front to partially cover his eyes. There was a slight scar on his left cheek from when he had once been beaten. He touched the scar gingerly, remembering the pain, but the pain that the injury had caused had long since passed. Jimmy turned his head to look at himself sideways. He was slim, which didn't surprise him due to his constant lack of food. He glanced away, not wanting to look at himself any longer. He gazed down at the floor thoughtfully, then looked up and crossed the small bedroom to the window to gaze outside. He saw the park across the road on the opposite side of the street and next to that he saw the graveyard. He stood for a moment, watching the people in the park and thinking of the very pretty and golden-haired girl, Rebecca's friend. He thought about what she and the other tall girl had said. It didn't seem to matter to Jimmy what the golden-haired girl had said about him, for him, she was still the most beautiful girl he had ever seen. He thought about speaking to her, about holding her hand, about kissing her forehead, about her looking at him and smiling, and then Rebecca came into his mind. She too was pretty, with her black shoulder-length hair, but she wasn't like the golden-haired girl, Jimmy thought. Nobody was.

He lay down on the bed feeling a soft pillow beneath his head for the first time since he had run away from his last foster parents at the age of ten. He closed his eyes and began to drift off into a deep, deep sleep.

CHAPTER 7

Jimmy awoke with a start.

It was now dark.

He heard voices whispering.

He sat up listening to the whispers but couldn't make out any words. The whispering seemed to be coming from outside his door. He stood up from the bed and moved slowly across the room to the door, the floorboards creaking beneath his feet as he went. He reached for the door handle, and then, just as he grasped it, the whispering stopped. He waited a moment, listening, then turned the handle and opened the door. He leaned forward and looked outside into the corridor. It was completely empty. He remained still listening but only heard a silence. Considering there were other people in the building, probably like himself, Jimmy thought that it was strange. Strange that he didn't hear anything, not a thing. He decided to go exploring. The corridor outside his room was long. He looked towards the right and saw that the corridor stretched to a closed door at the end. Jimmy stepped out of his room, closing the door gently behind him, and into the corridor. He paused glancing both right and left, and then began walking along it to the right towards the closed door. He listened as he went, not hearing any sounds in the silence behind any of the doors that he passed. When he reached the door at the end, he found that it was unlocked. He pushed it open and went through it and found himself in a stairwell. Jimmy stopped. He remained still, listening once more. Suddenly, he heard a noise. It came from the floor above. He glanced up, listening carefully, then started to mount the stairs, going up them two at a time. The noise came again, this time louder as he neared the floor above, and then he reached the landing and stopped once again, listening and hesitating as he stared at the closed door to the fourth floor in front of him. Slowly, he reached towards the door's handle. The noise sounded again. Jimmy hesitated, then turned the handle and opened the door. The moment he opened it, he found himself bathed in a red light. The corridor on the fourth floor now stretched forward in front of him completely covered in a red glow from the light. Jimmy stepped forward into the red corridor, the door to the stairwell creaking slowly shut behind him. The noise was clear now. It was the noise of someone screaming and crying. Between the screams he heard voices begging, begging for someone to stop what they were doing, and then the same voices screamed out again. Someone was being hit, or beaten. The screaming stopped, but now Jimmy continued to hear someone crying and sobbing. Jimmy moved slowly along the corridor heading towards the sound. He stopped when he reached the door behind which the sound was coming and stood still, staring at it. The crying and sobbing sounds continued on the other side of the door as Jimmy reached forward to grasp the handle, and then he opened it. The door opened inwards, creaking on its hinges as it went. The scene Jimmy saw inside the room made him gasp in shock. Two young boys, possibly nine or ten years old, were bound naked over two separate desks and were being beaten with a long thin cane by Tony. The boys were crying and sobbing as Tony beat one on the backside and then the other, systematically bringing his arm down, which was wielding the cane, as hard as he could. Painful red stinging marks showed on the boys' backsides as they screamed and cried beneath the blows. Tony, who had heard the door creak open behind him, turned to see Jimmy standing in the open doorway and looking at him.

"What the hell are you doing here?" Tony growled, staring at Jimmy with cold beast-like eyes.

Jimmy stared back at him and at the long and thin cane that Tony was holding tightly in his right hand.

"Stop beating them!" Jimmy suddenly shouted.

Tony grinned at him, "You want to be next kid?" he said.

Without any hesitation, Jimmy ran forward.

"No!" he cried. "No! No!"

He hit Tony square on the jaw knocking a surprised Tony to the floor, next, Jimmy picked up the cane Tony had dropped and began hitting him and hitting him, again and again, all of the time shouting "No! No! No!" at the top of his lungs.

Tony lay on the floor covering his head, cowering from the blows which Jimmy was raining down on him. When Jimmy had exhausted his energy, he stared down at the cowering Tony, then threw the cane to the floor and turned to unbind the two naked boys who were still crying and sobbing from the sharp stinging pain which had been inflicted upon them. As he was untying their bonds, he heard a noise behind him and turned to see Dr. Schultz and Miss Wong standing in the open doorway watching him.

Jimmy stared at Dr. Schultz and pointed down at Tony who was still lying on the floor.

"He ... he was beating them!" Jimmy said.

Dr. Shultz entered the room followed by Miss Wong behind him.

"I know," Dr. Schultz said. He held up a syringe in his right hand, "I told him to," he said.

Jimmy's eyes widened in surprise as he stared at the doctor.

Suddenly, Dr. Shultz leapt forward and plunged the syringe into Jimmy's neck. Jimmy cried out, and then immediately his head started to spin. The doctor stood watching as Jimmy staggered back and then fell unconscious to the floor.

Dr. Schultz smiled, gazing down at him, then turned to Miss Wong, "Put him in the pit for now," he said.

CHAPTER 8

Rebecca walked through the park towards the building with her two friends. Her golden-haired friend stopped walking beside her and sat down on a park bench. The tall brown-haired girl stopped walking too and hesitated, not sure if she should sit down with her friend or continue walking with her other friend, Rebecca. Rebecca turned and looked down at her friend on the bench.

"Aren't you coming?" Rebecca asked.

The golden-haired girl shook her head, "No! We'll wait here for you." She glanced at her tall brown-haired friend, "Right Ruth?"

Ruth glanced nervously from her golden-haired friend to Rebecca.

"Ellie," Rebecca said, looking down at the golden-haired girl, "come on! It'll only take a few minutes!"

Elli looked up at her, "No way!" she said. "You're the one who wants go around helping tramps! The one who used to do voluntary work in that place, not us!"

She glanced at her tall friend, Ruth, who was staring at her, "Come on Ruth, sit down with me! We'll wait here together."

Ruth, the tall girl, continued to hesitate.

"I ... I don't know," she said. "Maybe just once, we could go in and have a look, see what it's like."

Rebecca looked at her, "Thank you Ruth," she said. She glanced back down at Ellie who had now taken out her mobile phone and began surfing on the internet.

"Ellie'" Rebecca said, "I just want you to see the 'real' world for once. Not the world inside that computer of yours."

"I like the computer world," Ellie said. "It's clean, it's fun, and I enjoy it!"

Ruth looked at Rebecca, "You know how stubborn she is," Ruth said with a shrug.

Rebecca stepped towards the bench, "Ellie, please, just for once, come and see these people."

Ellie shook her head studying something on the screen of her mobile phone, "I've seen them," she said. "On the streets, in the parks! They're dirty! Disgusting! I don't want anything to do with them! You go ahead if you want to, but I'm staying right here!"

Rebecca sighed, "Okay then, wait here."

She turned to her friend Ruth, "Ruth, are you coming?"

Ruth nodded, "Just this once," she said. "I'll come to see where you did your voluntary work."

Rebecca smiled, "okay," she said, "let's go."

Ellie remained sitting on the bench and surfing on her mobile phone.

"Be back soon!" Rebecca called back, as both she and Ruth continued to walk along the path.

Ellie, who was now completely absorbed by something on her mobile phone, merely grunted without looking up.

Dr. Schultz greeted Rebecca with his usual smile as Rebecca introduced him to her friend Ruth.

"How's Jimmy settling in?" Rebecca asked.

"Ah ... well ... yes ... we've had a little problem with Jimmy," Dr. Schultz said. "We had to sedate him. He's been taken to the special wing."

"The special wing?" Rebecca repeated, staring at the doctor in surprise.

When she was a voluntary worker for her school project, Rebecca had heard of the special wing. It was the part of the building reserved for violent or serious problem cases. All the time she had worked there, Rebecca had never been allowed to set foot in the special wing.

"I ... I'm surprised!" Rebecca said. "He ... he seemed like such a gentle boy, very shy."

"Yes, well, appearances can be deceiving. Disorientation can be disturbing sometimes," Dr. Schultz said. "There's no telling what goes through the head of someone like Jimmy, at least, not yet."

"Well ... can I see him?" Rebecca asked. "Maybe I can talk to him, try to help him to calm down."

Dr. Shultz glanced at Ruth who was walking around the doctor's office looking at the photos on the walls.

"My dear," he said, looking back to Rebecca, "we're doing everything we can, believe me. I'm afraid the special wing is off limits except for specialized personnel, as I'm sure you remember."

Rebecca glanced down with a sigh, then nodded, "Yes, I remember," she said.

Dr. Shultz glanced once again at Ruth, "Are you interested in being a voluntary worker here as well?" he asked.

Ruth turned and smiled at him, "Oh, no ... sorry, I ... I'm just here to accompany Rebecca. She told me what you do here, helping these people, taking them in off the streets."

She pointed at the photos on the walls, "Are these some of the people you've helped?" she asked.

Dr. Schultz nodded, "Some of them," he said. "Some were helpers, like Rebecca once was. Some needed medical care, others needed psychological help."

"And Jimmy?" Rebecca asked.

Dr. Schultz glanced down thoughtfully, "He has psychological problems," he said. "But rest assured, with care, and patience, he can be cured."

Rebecca nodded, "I see."

Dr. Shultz smiled, "Maybe you'd like to show your friend Ruth around?"

He looked at Ruth, "Maybe you could become one of our voluntary workers," he said. "As Rebecca here can tell you, helping people can be rewarding."

Ruth returned the doctor's smile, "Thank you doctor, but I'm just looking. I just wanted to see what kind of voluntary work my friend Rebecca was doing here."

"Of course," Dr. Schultz said. "Please feel free to visit."

As they were about to leave the doctor spoke to Rebecca, "Er ... Rebecca. Remember, not the special wing. It ... er ... could be dangerous."

Rebecca nodded, "Okay doctor, no problem."

Dr. Schultz smiled and saw them out of his office.

*

Jimmy woke up.

He was in a small dark room.

He tried to remember what had happened and then remembered the two boys being beaten. He remembered seeing Dr. Schultz, and then everything went black. He stood up and looked around the dark room he was in. There was a small red light glowing on the wall far above him. He quickly noticed that there was nothing in the room, no furniture, not even one chair or a bed. It was as if he was in a box. He glanced up, and then realized that he was in some kind of pit or hole. In the dim red light that glowed from the wall he saw what looked like a door high above him. There was no way he could get to it, he'd need a ladder. He stared at the glowing red light, then walked around touching the walls. They were old, cold and clammy from a dampness. Where was he? Why was he put here? The questions burned in his head as he tried to find some grip on the walls so that he could climb up. After some minutes of trying, he finally gave up and sat on the floor. He would wait, he thought, he would have to wait, until they came for him. And then what would happen? he wondered. Would they want to punish him too? Like they did the two little boys? But he was no longer a child. He was a teenager and more determined than when he was younger. When they came for him, he would fight. Yes, he thought to himself. I'm not a child. This time, I will fight them, this time ... I will fight back!

CHAPTER 9

Rebecca showed Ruth to a long room that was part of the west wing of the building. There were rows of beds on both sides of the room. It reminded Ruth of a hospital with a large ward. A few people lay on some of the beds resting, while others sat on chairs drinking something hot or playing on computers. The people were a mixture of old, young or middle-aged, but there were no children.

"Wow!" Ruth said as she looked at them. "Everyone's got a computer!"

Rebecca nodded, "The doctor believes an interest in computers can stimulate them. They can either watch films, play games or chat online with people outside."

"A great idea!" Ruth said, walking along the centre aisle with Rebecca at her side.

"So, what did you do as a volunteer?" Ruth asked.

Rebecca shrugged, "Oh, I helped cook, serve meals, I made sure they were clean, chatted to them, although they didn't seem to want to chat much, they were too interested in the computers."

Ruth laughed, "Oh, so they became computer addicts, just like Ellie!" she said.

"And like you," Rebecca said, glancing at her friend. "You and Ellie are alike, you both love going online!"

"Hey! I'm here aren't I?" Ruth said in defense. "Okay, so I like going online, but Ellie is much worse than me!

Rebecca laughed, "Yes, I guess you're right!" she said.

Suddenly Rebecca noticed a small boy standing in front of the far door staring at them. She stopped walking and looked at him in surprise. She had never seen children in the building before. The boy had very pale skin, almost white. His large dark brown eyes stared at them piercingly.

Ruth glanced at Rebecca, "What is it?" she asked.

"That boy," Rebecca said. "The way he's ... staring at us."

Ruth turned to look in the direction that Rebecca was looking.

"What boy?" she asked, seeing nothing.

"The boy, just by the door," Rebecca said..

Ruth looked again towards the door.

"There's no one there," she said. "Are you sure you're not imagining things?"

"But ... he's there!" Rebecca said, pointing her finger at the boy. "He ... he's right there!"

The boy raised his arm and made a gesture for Rebecca to follow him.

"Er ... are you sure you're okay?" Ruth said, studying Rebecca with a concerned look on her face.

The boy turned and went through the door leaving the room.

"He wants us to follow him!" Rebecca said.

"Rebecca! There's no one there!" Ruth said.

"There 'was' a boy!" Rebecca said. "There was! Come on!"

She started to walk fast towards the door.

"We have to follow him!"

Ruth watched her moving towards the door.

"This is crazy!" she said under her breath, then began to follow after her.

*

Jimmy sat in the dimly red-lit small room, which to him seemed more like a pit. As he sat, wondering when they would come for him, he began to hear voices whispering again. He looked around and then looked up at the closed door high above him. The whispering voices seemed to be just nearby him. Jimmy stood up. He listened, trying to distinguish exactly what the voices were saying. He moved to the wall and placed his ear against it trying to determine where the whispering was coming from, then he walked around the small room, each time placing his ear against the walls. The whispering grew louder. The voices seemed to be all around him and not located in any one place. He spun around looking at the walls, listening to the voices and trying to understand what they were saying, but try as he might, he could distinguish no words.

Suddenly, the whispering stopped.

Silence.

He glanced up at the dim red light glowing above far above him. And then he heard voices, this time voices speaking, not whispering.

Jimmy looked up towards the closed door, the voices were coming from above.

*

"Are you sure we're not going to get into trouble?" Ruth said to Rebecca. "The doctor told us not to go into the special wing!"

Rebecca was watching the pale-skinned small boy as he led her along a corridor and into a room on the right. The room was dimly-lit. Only one fading light-bulb shone from the ceiling above. Rebecca watched as the small boy walked over to a door and then turned to her and pointed towards it. Rebecca stared at him, stifling a gasp. The boy's skin seemed to be glowing white in the semi-darkness of the room.

"What is it now?" Ruth asked, stopping beside her.

"It's the boy!" Rebecca said. "He ... he's pointing to that door! He ... he's skin seems to be glowing!"

Ruth looked at the door that Rebecca was now pointing towards.

"Rebecca, there is no one there!" Ruth said. "Look, I don't know what's going on with you, but you're beginning to freak me out!"

Suddenly Rebecca gasped again, holding her hand to her mouth, her eyes open wide in shock.

"What is it now?" Ruth asked, staring at her friend curiously.

"The ... the boy!" Rebecca said, pointing towards the door. "He ... he just ... disappeared! Vanished! He ... he was there! And now ... he's gone!"

Ruth placed a hand on Rebecca's head, "I think you must have a fever!" she said. "You're seeing things!"

"No!" Rebecca said, walking towards the door, her hands were now shaking.

"Look! The doctor said we shouldn't be here!" Ruth said, glancing around worriedly. "Let's go now, before we get into trouble! Besides, this place is beginning to give me the creeps!'"

But Rebecca had already reached the door.

Slowly, she raised her hand towards the door's handle. Her hand still shaking as she grasped it. She hesitated, and then turned it.

The door was locked.

"We have to open it!" Rebecca said, turning to Ruth.

Ruth stared at her, "Are you crazy! There might be a mad killer behind that door for all we know!"

Rebecca glanced around for something to force the door open. In the dim light, she saw a small metal box on the wall beside the door. She opened it and felt inside. When she brought her hand back out, she was holding a key. It was a long key, the type that fitted old locks. She glanced at Ruth, who was watching her with wide fearful eyes, then turned back to the door and placed the key into the lock.

"Rebecca!" Ruth said sharply. "No!"

But Rebecca had already turned the key in the lock. She heard a click. She remained still for a moment, then took a deep breath and opened the door.

CHAPTER 10

In the silence, the door creaked as Rebecca opened it slowly.

Jimmy, who was sitting on the floor, looked up hearing the creaking of the opening door far above him. He stood up, bunching his hands into fists, ready to fight whoever came down to grab him.

Rebecca almost stepped forward and managed to stop herself just in time with a gasp. She glanced down and saw the dim red light glowing on the wall. Peering into the darkness below it, she made out a shape. Someone was down there.

"Hello?" she called out. "Hello?"

Jimmy recognized Rebecca's voice as he gazed upwards.

"Rebecca?" he called out.

"Jimmy?" Rebecca called down in surprise. "Jimmy? Is that you?"

"Yes!" Jimmy replied. "R ... Rebecca! C ... can you get me out?" he said, stuttering as he spoke.

Ruth placed a hand on Rebecca's arm, "Don't do it!" she said. "He has to be down there for a reason! Maybe he's dangerous!"

Rebecca turned to her.

"Ruth, he's in some kind of dark pit! I mean ... who does that?"

"Rebecca! No!" Ruth said. "He could be dangerous! We don't know what he's capable of!"

Rebecca took Ruth's hand off her arm.

"We have to get him out!" she said.

"Rebecca!" Ruth said, watching as Rebecca looked around the room they were in.

Rebecca saw something leaning against the far wall and ran over to it. It was a ladder. She picked it up and took it back over towards the open door and the pit.

"Rebecca!" Ruth said, stepping between her and the open door. "No! ... Don't do it Rebecca! He's down there for a reason!"

Rebecca looked at her, "Nobody ..." she said, "nobody deserves to be treated like that! Nobody!"

Ruth grasped her arm, "Rebecca! You found him on the street! He's a nobody! A nobody! He's not worth getting into trouble for!"

Rebecca pulled away from Ruth's hand.

She stared at her friend.

"If that's what you think, then go! Go on! Go! As for me, I'm going to help him!"

Ruth stared back at her, then sighed, "You really are stubborn!" she said.

Rebecca moved the ladder through the door, then placed it down over the pit and began to lower it down. When it reached the bottom, Jimmy began to climb up it. Both Rebecca and Ruth watched as Jimmy reached the top and stepped out of the pit and into the room where they were standing. Ruth took a few steps back staring at him. Rebecca also stared at him, surprised at his transformation. Jimmy now looked clean, and with his haircut, even younger than before.

"What happened?" Rebecca asked. "Why were you down there?'

Jimmy glanced down, as if he were embarrassed "I ... I hit someone," he said.

Ruth took a few more steps back away from him.

"Rebecca ..." she said softly as she continued to stare at Jimmy.

"I ... I hit a worker named Tony," Jimmy continued. "He ... he was beating two boys. I ... I couldn't stand to see that."

"Two boys?" Rebecca repeated.

Jimmy nodded, keeping his head lowered, not daring to look into either of the girls' eyes..

Rebecca stared at him, "I ... I understand," she said, after a moment. "The doctor had no right to put you in that ... that pit!"

"There ... there's something strange here," Jimmy said.

"S ... something's not quite right," he stuttered.

"Okay," Rebecca said. "Look, we'll get you out."

"If they're beating children and putting people in pits," Ruth said, now looking at her friend, "maybe we should go to the police."

Rebecca nodded, "You're right."

She touched Jimmy's arm gently, "Let's go," she said.

"But ... the boys!" Jimmy said, with a worried look on his face. "We ... we can't leave them! We have to get them out too!"

"The police will take care of that," Rebecca said. "Come on, we have to go now."

Reluctantly, Jimmy nodded, "Okay," he said.

Jimmy followed the two girls towards the door that led them back out into the corridor. As they entered the corridor and started walking along it, Ruth moved closer to Rebecca and whispered into her ear.

"I thought you said there were no children here."

Rebecca nodded, "Usually not," she whispered back.

"I don't trust him," Ruth whispered. "What if he's lying?"

"R ... Rebecca?" Jimmy said, before Rebecca could whisper an answer back to Ruth.

Rebecca turned to look at him.

"Th ... thanks," Jimmy said. "Thanks for ... for getting me out."

Rebecca smiled at him, "It's okay," she said.

Together they continued along the corridor. The corridor was empty and strangely silent. They had almost reached the end when they heard voices coming from another corridor which branched to the right. The three of them stopped in their tracks.

"This way!" Rebecca said, pulling on Jimmy's arm.

Ruth followed as Rebecca led them back along the corridor towards another corridor branching to their left. Just as they were about to enter the other corridor, Miss Wong and a male worker appeared and saw them.

"Stop them!" Miss Wong cried out pointing towards them.

The male worker, another big man, ran forward along the corridor towards them, shouting out as he ran. Rebecca and the others turned the corner entering the corridor to their left.

"Stop! Stop!" the man called out as he ran after them, turning the corner into the corridor on the left behind them. The three teenagers ran along the corridor as fast as they could and burst through the swing doors at the far end with the male worker in hot pursuit.

Miss Wong took out her mobile phone and speed dialed Dr. Schultz's number.

"We have a problem," she said into the phone.

CHAPTER 11

Rebecca ran through the swing doors into another corridor followed by Jimmy and Ruth. Suddenly, the three of them stopped.

They gazed at the corridor in front of them in surprise. The corridor was bathed in a strange blue light, but what was surprising about it was that it was crooked. The floor rose up on the left and down on the right as if something had tilted it to one side. The three of them stared at the corridor with open mouths. Footsteps sounded in the other corridor behind them.

"He's coming!" Ruth said.

Rebecca ran forward, fighting to keep her balance on the tilted floor. She reached the first door on the right and turned the handle. It was unlocked.

"In here!" she called back to the others.

Both Jimmy and Ruth followed Rebecca across the tilted floor and through the open door. Rebecca quickly closed it behind them when they were through and stood listening at the door. They heard the footsteps of the male worker who was chasing them pass by in the corridor outside and continue along it.

When the footsteps had disappeared, Rebecca turned to look back at the others. The room was completely bathed in a red light.

Both Jimmy and Ruth were standing still and staring at something in the room's centre. Rebecca stepped forward to follow their gaze. After taking a few steps, she saw what they were staring at and gasped in surprise. In the centre of the room, there was the body of a man. He was possibly in his thirties and was completely naked, but what was special about him was the fact that he was suspended in mid-air as if he were somehow floating and facing downwards about four feet above the floor.

"Wha ... what's going on?" Ruth said, staring wide-eyed at the man's suspended body.

Rebecca stepped forward towards him.

"I ... I don't know," she said, staring at the man's body with a look of shock on her face.

Jimmy moved forward past her to stand beside the man's suspended body. He ran his hands about a foot over the man's body and beneath it.

"He ... he's suspended ... in ... in mid-air!" Jimmy said.

"How's that possible?" Ruth asked, staring at the man's suspended body in shock. "Is ... is he alive?" she asked.

"He doesn't ... seem to be breathing," Rebecca said, still staring at him.

Ruth took a step back from the man's body and looked at the others.

"Wha ... what the hell's going on here?" she asked, suddenly very afraid. "Wha ... what's happening? What is this?"

Rebecca looked at her and shook her head, "I don't know," she said. "I know as much as you do."

"You ... you're the one who worked here!" Ruth said, staring at her. "You ... you're the one who saw the ... the ghost! Or whatever it was!"

Rebecca crouched down to observe the man's body from underneath, then turned to face her, "Look, Ruth, I'm as mystified as you are! I ... I've never been to this part of the building before!"

Jimmy glanced at them both.

"Look ... er ... maybe we ... we should just find a way out, okay?"

Rebecca looked at him, then nodded, "You're right," she said, standing up.

"Oh, you are so definitely right!" Ruth said with a shaky voice.

Jimmy pointed to the left, "There's another door over there," he said.

Rebecca nodded looking towards the door, "Okay, let's try it," she said.

Both Jimmy and Rebecca walked across the red room towards the door followed by Ruth who was now visibly shaking with fear.

"I ... I really hope there's not another body behind that door!" Ruth said as she turned away from the man's suspended body to follow them..

"We'll find out," Rebecca said, reaching for the door's handle. She hesitated, then took a deep breath, grasped the handle and turned it slowly.

Each of them tensed as Rebecca paused before opening the door, then she pushed it open. In front of them was a narrow passage bathed in a green light. They stared at it, looked at each other, then stepped forward into it and closed the door behind them.

"Where do you think it leads?" Ruth asked in a trembling voice.

Neither Rebecca nor Jimmy answered her. The three of them walked along the narrow passage towards the other end. After going about ten feet, it turned to the left. It continued for about another ten feet then twisted to the right. They continued on along the passage in silence following its twist and turns. After a few minutes, they came to a door.

"This place really gives me the creeps!" Ruth said, as they neared the door.

She took out a mobile phone and dialed a number.

"What are you doing?" Rebecca asked.

"What does it look like I'm doing?" Ruth answered. "I'm calling the police!"

She looked back down at her phone.

"Oh great!" she exclaimed. "No signal!"

Rebecca took out her phone and checked it.

"Mine's the same," she said. "I guess we'll just have to find a way out without getting caught."

She looked at the door in front of them, then sighed.

"Another door," she said.

Jimmy stepped forward, "I'll do it," he said.

He reached for the handle, turned it slowly, and then pushed it forward.

This next room was completely black.

"I can't see a thing!" Rebecca said, gazing into the next room.

Ruth stepped back away from the open door.

"I ... I'm not going in there!" she said, shaking her head. "No way! ... No way!"

Rebecca glanced back at her.

"Maybe there's another door on the other side," she said. "We can't go back."

Ruth shook her head again staring at the pitch blackness in front of her.

"No!" she said.

Rebecca raised her hand towards her, "Come on, take my hand, we'll do this together."

Ruth stared down at Rebecca's hand.

"Come on," Rebecca urged with a smile. "We'll soon be out of this place."

Ruth continued to stare at Rebecca's hand trying to summon up her courage. She took a deep breath, then finally stepped forward and took Rebecca's hand. Rebecca turned to Jimmy and held out her other hand towards him.

"We go together," she said.

Jimmy nodded, then grasped her outstretched hand. Rebecca took a deep breath, then stepped forward into the pitch black room with Ruth and Jimmy on either side of her. For a few moments, they walked ahead very slowly, hearing absolutely no sound as they did so, then suddenly, they felt something nearby them, a strange energy that seemed to draw them on almost as if they were caught up in some kind of electrical wind.

The next moment, Rebecca cried out.

She fell, taking the others with her, each of them crying out and screaming at the top of their lungs as they fell downwards into what seemed like a huge black hole that had appeared in the floor beneath them. They fell and fell and fell, screaming as they went, wondering if they were going to die when they finally reached the bottom.

CHAPTER 12

They screamed!

"Aaaaaargh!"

And then they fell out of the darkness and into the light, hitting and rolling on the grassy land below them.

The three of them lay still for a few moments, panting with eyes tightly closed, wondering if they were injured or dead. Jimmy was the first to open his eyes. He sat up, gazing around, then he pulled himself up onto his feet staring at the scene before him in total disbelief. He was standing on a grassy slope. The slope led down to a beach, and there, he saw the ocean, its waves crashing up onto the bright yellow sand below him. The sky above looked dark, stormy, and far towards the horizon, he saw lightning streaking down. Rebecca stirred beside him and stood up. She gazed at the scene in front of her open-mouthed.

"Where the hell are we?" she said, as if speaking to herself.

"I ... I don't know," Jimmy said, shaking his head as he watched the lightning streaking down from the dark clouds on the far horizon. "One minute, we were in a building in the city, miles away from ... from the ocean," he said, "and now ..."

Rebecca stared at the ocean and at the storm in the distance.

"I ... I just ... don't believe this!" she said in amazement.

Ruth, still lying on the ground a few feet away, glanced up at them and then began to pull herself up onto her feet.

"Did ... did we find the way out?" she asked, not yet seeing the scenery in front of them.

Rebecca nodded, continuing to stare at the distant storm.

"You could say that," she said.

Ruth, now standing up, looked around.

She saw the beach, she saw the ocean, and then she saw the distant storm.

"What the hell ... !" she exclaimed, in open-mouthed shock.

"Whe ... where the hell are we? What happened? How ... how did we get here?"

Jimmy turned to look at her, then glanced back at the distant storm.

"We'd better find some shelter," he said, "before the storm hits."

"Yes, but ... where the hell are we?" Ruth shouted again from behind him.

Jimmy turned, looked up at the slope behind them, then moved past Ruth and started to climb up the slope to the top.

"Where are you going?" Ruth shouted, staring at him.

"To find out where we are!" Jimmy called back.

Rebecca looked away from the approaching storm and back up towards Jimmy.

"He's right," she said, stepping past Ruth to climb up the slope behind him. "We have to find out where we are."

Ruth stood watching on the side of the slope as both Jimmy and Rebecca climbed up towards the top.

"This is crazy!" she shouted up at them.

She glanced back towards the sea and the storm, then turned to follow them up.

Jimmy reached the top of the slope and stood looking down over the other side. He remained still, staring, as Rebecca joined him.

"Oh my God!" Rebecca exclaimed, as saw what was on the other side of the slope.

CHAPTER 13

Both Jimmy and Rebecca stood on top of the slope staring down.

There, below them, they saw strange looking beings. They had human forms, but they were obviously not human. Their faces were completely different, They looked like some kind of monsters with strange grey skin. They seemed to be wearing a purple uniform with armor, and helmets with horns rising from them. They were also carrying long spear-like weapons, which, instead of having one pointed tip, had two, as it separated at the end. They seemed to be soldiers or guards, and they were standing on either side of a large column of other beings who were moving slowly through a field, most of them with their heads lowered.. These ones were different, mixed, some human-like, some short like dwarfs, others were totally different. They walked, or rather, trudged along between their guards as if they were prisoners.

Ruth came up the slope joining both Jimmy and Rebecca and gazed down at the scene below in wide-eyed shock.

"What the hell ... !" she exclaimed once again to herself.

Suddenly, one of the guards turned and saw them. He cried out in a language they could not understand and then other guards turned to look at them.

"Er ... I think it's time to go!" Rebecca said urgently, as she saw a few of the guards leave the prison column to run towards them.

Jimmy nodded, "Run!" he shouted.

Rebecca grabbed Ruth's hand as Ruth remained staring down at the scene below in complete shock.

"Come on!" Rebecca shouted, pulling the shocked Ruth behind her.

They ran back down the slope towards the beach, then ran along it, hearing the approaching storm to their right, and the shouts of the strange looking creatures now mounting to the top of the slope to their left.

*

Ellie glanced at her watch.

It was getting late.

She wondered just when the hell her friends, Rebecca and Ruth, were coming back. She felt a cold breeze and pulled her jacket up around her throat, then she looked back down and continued with what she was doing on her mobile phone. It seemed to be getting colder. The cold breeze now seemed to be turning into a strong wind. Ellie glanced up and then saw the clouds. The clouds were dark, almost black as they rolled strangely across the sky. A lightning bolt shot down from them followed by a loud boom of thunder. Ellie stood up, staring up at the rolling black clouds that were coming fast across the sky. There was something strange about them, she thought, as she gazed up at them, something ...

Lightning flashed again and struck the roof of the large dark red building which Rebecca and Ruth had gone to. The black clouds now seemed to be building up in the sky above and around the building. Ellie continued to stare up at them, and then she heard it, a voice calling her name. She stared towards the now ominous-looking dark red building and shivered involuntarily. Suddenly, her eyes glazed over, and then slowly she began to walk stiffly along the park's path towards the building as if she were sleepwalking or in some kind of trance. Across the park, just by the trees and not far from the graveyard, a small pale boy watched Ellie walking through the park towards the building. Various voices seemed to whisper among the trees around him as he watched Ellie with a fixed stare, and then, the next moment, he disappeared.

*

Rebecca ran through the trees of a forest she had reached followed by both Ruth and Jimmy. She stopped and leaned against a tree breathing heavily, "Do you think we lost them?" she asked.

"I don't know,' Jimmy said, stopping beside her.

"Let's take a breather!" Ruth said, falling against a tree, completely out of breath. "Please!"

"Look!" Jimmy said, parting the bushes to their right and pointing.

Both Rebecca and Ruth looked through the bushes.

"Wha ... what are they doing?" Ruth asked, peering through the bushes at a field on the other side.

Together, they watched as a long line of prisoners flanked by guards were being taken to what looked like a very large triangular screen in the middle of the field. There were steps leading up to a platform just in front of the screen, and when they reached it, two waiting guards pushed them over one large step and the prisoners entered inside. Jimmy and the others stared at the large triangular screen and saw what appeared to be another world inside it. Jimmy realized that what they were looking at was not really a screen, but a gateway, a portal leading from one world and into another.

"My God!" Ruth gasped. "What the hell is that?"

"I've no idea!" Rebecca said. "And I don't want to hang around to find out! The people they're herding into that thing are prisoners! Whatever it is, it's not good!"

"It's a gateway into another world," Jimmy said, almost to himself as he stared at the large triangular object.

Both Rebecca and Ruth stared at him.

"A gateway?" Rebecca repeated..

"It's the only thing that makes sense," Jimmy said.

"Nothing makes sense!" Ruth said, looking at him. "This is all ... completely crazy!"

Suddenly, they heard a noise behind them.

All three instantly spun round.

A short grey-bearded man was standing behind them and staring up at them. He looked like a dwarf. He placed a finger to his lips for them to be quiet.

"Shhhh!" he whispered.

The three stared back down at him in surprise. He was wearing ancient-looking clothes which seemed to belong to a century at least a thousand years in the past. The man pointed to his left and through the bushes they saw the approaching guards who had been running after them. They froze, remaining still and quiet as they guards moved through the trees and bushes speaking a strange language. They crouched down, watching the guards pass, and then, when the guards were sufficiently far away, they looked back down at the short bearded man. He was now staring up at them with a smile on his face and cocking his head to one side as if he were both surprised and amused at seeing them. He observed them carefully, studying what, for him, were strange clothes.

"Where are you from?" he asked.

Rebecca stepped forward staring down at him, as amazed by his appearance as he was by theirs.

"You ... speak English?" she asked.

The small man stared up at her in surprise, his eyes opening wider.

"English? What's that?"

"It's ... our language," Rebecca said, now even more surprised by his question.

"Oh! Yes!" he said, now understanding her question. "Language? Yes! Yes! I ... I suppose I do! Or rather ... you speak Getriese!"

"Getriese?" Rebecca repeated, gazing down at him in confusion.

"Yes! Yes! Language! My language! It is what I am speaking now!"

"No ... " Rebecca said slowly. "You ... you're speaking English!"

The little man giggled, then shrugged, "Well, if you wish!" he said.

Jimmy stepped forward, "Where are we?" he asked. "I mean ... one minute we were in ... in one place, and now ..."

"And now you are here!" the little man giggled again. "Confusing, isn't it?"

A strong wind blew through the leaves of the trees and the surrounding bushes, rustling them.

"Storm coming!" the little man said. "You come! You come with me! Must get to shelter!"

The three of them watched as the little man turned and started to walk back through the bushes. Suddenly, the little man stopped and turned back to them as they remained still, staring at him.

"You come!" he called. "Storm is not good! This place dangerous! You come! You come now!"

He gestured for them to follow him, then turned and once again began walking back through the bushes. Rebecca glanced at both Jimmy and Ruth, then turned back and began to follow the little man through the woods with Jimmy and Ruth following close behind her.

CHAPTER 14

Ellie stood still in a darkened room. She stared straight ahead as if she were in a hypnotic state.

Miss Wong moved forward into a shaft of light to look at her.

"Do you think it is wise to send her through?" Miss Wong asked.

Dr. Schultz stepped into the light to stand beside her. He studied Ellie in front of him, staring at her glazed eyes.

"It should be no problem," he said. "She is Rebecca's friend, Rebecca trusts her."

"Why don't we just forget about them?" Miss Wong asked. "Where they are now, they can't harm us."

Dr. Schultz turned to her, "On the contrary, we must leave nothing to chance. They have proved to be resourceful. We will send this one through. She will make sure that nothing disturbs our plans."

Miss Wong nodded, "As you wish doctor."

Dr. Shultz smiled as he stared at Ellie, then gestured towards an open door.

"You may enter the Darkness my dear," he said.

Ellie, upon hearing the doctor's command, stepped forward towards the open door and disappeared into the darkness of the room on the other side.

*

As they walked, the little man turned to them and introduced himself as Roe.

"Row?" Rebecca laughed. "That's what people do in a boat!"

Roe turned to glare back at her with a less than amused expression.

"And what is your name?" he asked, in an obviously vexed tone as they continued walking through the forest.

"My name's Rebecca," Rebecca answered. "And these are my friends, Ruth and Jimmy."

"Ah!" the little man said with a smile, "Reb, Ru and Jee."

"No ..." Rebecca said. "Rebecca, Ruth and Jimmy."

Roe stopped walking and turned to face her.

"In this world," he said, "we like short names. Reb, Ru and Jee, they are good names."

Rebecca sighed, staring down at him.

"It seems like everything's short in this world!" Ruth said, looking down at him.

Roe glanced up at her angrily, "Does the giant, Ru, feel herself superior perhaps?" he said to her.

"Giant?" Ruth repeated, moving towards him. "Okay, I'm tall! But I'm no giant!" she said, slightly annoyed at being called a giant.

"To me, you are a giant!" Roe said, staring up at her. "That is the problem with giants!" he added. "They always feel superior!"

Rebecca stepped between them, "Hey! My friend, Ruth ... er ... Ru ... didn't mean anything, okay?'

"Hummph!" Roe snorted, then turned to continue on through the forest.

"Sensitive, isn't he?" Ruth said, looking at Rebecca.

Rebecca sighed, "Let's not create anymore problems than we already have. At least, he's helping us," she said.

Ruth nodded, "Okay," she said, raising her eyebrows. "Sorry."

"I wonder where we're going," Jimmy said.

Rebecca looked up at the dark sky. Lightning flashed above them and thunder boomed and rumbled loudly.

"Wherever it is, we'd better get there fast!" she said.

They continued on for a few minutes, and then suddenly, they exited the trees and stood on the edge of a clearing. On the opposite side was a rocky hillside sloping up.

"We are here!" Roe said, glancing round at them.

He pointed towards a small opening at the base of a rock which looked like an entrance to a cave. Just then, it began to rain hard.

"Come! Quickly!" Roe shouted, running forward across the clearing towards the opening in the rock wall. The others ran through the pouring rain behind him and then entered the opening pulling at their wet clothes. They looked around and saw that the cave-like entrance led through to a narrow passage.

"This way!" Roe said, gesturing them on.

They glanced at each other, then began to follow Roe along the passage. As they walked, sometimes having to crouch down along the way, they found that various stones and rocks glowed on either side of the passage illuminating their way as the passage twisted and turned in front of them. Finally, the passage widened, and then they found themselves in a wide underground cavern. At least forty people were there. Some of them were sitting on rocks, others were sitting in small groups on the ground. All of them were as short as Roe and were dressed in the same ancient-styled clothing. Everyone suddenly stopped talking as Roe entered the large cavern followed by Rebecca, Jimmy and Ruth.

"Look what I found!" Roe cried out, as he walked towards them.

A small man, who'd been sitting on a rock, stood up. This one was younger than Roe with a brown beard.

"You bring strangers?" the man said. "Here?"

"Relax Tol," Roe said calmly, holding out his arms. "They were being hunted! Their enemies are our enemies!"

The small man called Tol stepped forward angrily.

"Hunted?" he said. "They will search everywhere!"

"As they have searched before," Roe said, approaching him. "And yet, they never find us, right?"

"Their magic is strong!" Tol said. "One day they will!"

"Then we must make sure our magic is stronger!" Roe said.

He looked at the surrounding people who were staring at Rebecca, Jimmy and Ruth curiously.

"This is Reb!" Roe called out, gesturing to Rebecca. "And this is Jee! And the giant there ... " he pointed at Ruth, "that's Ru!"

He glanced back at the people, "They need our help! Do you want to turn them away? Turn them over to the 'Darkness'?"

The short people mumbled among themselves.

Suddenly, a short woman stood up. She had grey hair like Roe.

"I welcome you!" she said.

She turned to the others.

"My husband Roe is right! We must all welcome them! Who among you would throw them out to be taken by the Darkness'?"

All of the people in the cavern stared at her in silence. The woman looked at Tol, "Tol! Your family was taken by the Darkness'! Would you wish that on others?" she asked.

Tol looked back at her, then glanced down as if he were ashamed.

"No, Sev ... you are right, your husband is right. I ... I am sorry, I speak hastily."

He glanced back up at Rebecca, Jimmy and Ruth, "You are welcome!" he said, and tried a smile.

Rebecca felt the uneasiness of the people in the cavern and stepped forward.

She nodded and smiled back at Tol.

"Thank you," she said.

Then she looked at all of the other people gathered there.

"Thank you all," she said.

Sev, Roe's wife, nodded with a smile and gestured towards a long flat stone on which she had been sitting.

"Come!" she said. "Sit here!"

Tol stood to one side, watching, his smile fading, as the small group passed in front of him, heading towards the large flat stone.

"My! You are tall!" Sev said, staring up at Ruth as she sat down next to Rebecca and Jimmy.

Ruth smiled, "Not so much," she said. "At least, not where we come from."

"And where do you come from?" Sev asked.

"They come from another world," Roe said, sitting down on the large flat stone beside his wife. "I saw them arrive! They fell from the sky and landed near the beach! The Gools chased them and then they hid. That's when I approached them and brought them here."

"The Gools," Sev repeated, glancing down with a serious look. "There were more prisoners?"

"Many, many more." Roe replied. "I'm afraid they grow stronger with numbers ..."

"Excuse me," Rebecca said, leaning forward towards them, 'but ... can you tell us where we are? Who you are? Who these ... Gools are? What ... what is this place? And ... what's this ... this 'Darkness' you keep talking about?"

Both Sev and Roe stared at her.

"Oh my!" Sev said in surprise. "You really know nothing, do you?"

"They're as innocent as new-born babies!" Roe giggled.

His wife, Sev, shot him a glance, and Roe quickly looked down.

Sev turned back to Rebecca.

"How ... how did you arrive here, in our world?" she asked.

Rebecca glanced at both Jimmy and Ruth.

"We ... we were in a dark room," Jimmy said.

"Totally black!" Ruth added.

"And then ... we ... we fell through ... something ... something in the floor, kind of like a ... a hole," Jimmy continued.

Rebecca nodded, confirming what Jimmy had just said.

"We went through some kind of tunnel," she said. "And then ... we fell out and landed near the beach."

"A ... totally black room?" Sev asked, gazing at her intensely.

Rebecca nodded again, "We were ... " she sighed, as if she were about to say something that even she couldn't believe. "We were ... in our world, in a special place, a building where they look after people."

"Lost people," Jimmy added.

"Lost ... people?" Sev repeated, looking at him.

She glanced at her husband.

"They must have entered their world," she said.

Roe nodded thoughtfully, "They are expanding much faster than we thought," he said.

"Look!" Ruth said impatiently. "Would you please tell us where we are? Who are those Gools? And what the hell is the Darkness!"

Both Roe and his wife looked at her.

They remained silent for a moment, then Sev began to speak.

CHAPTER 15

"The Darkness came into our world many years ago," Sev said. "At first, dark clouds covered the sky, and there was a storm, an enormously strong storm. Then, the beings appeared, dark and evil. They were tall like you, but they could change shape. They could appear quite ordinary, or appear like ... like some nightmarish creature, a dark creature that uses magical powers to enslave others. We are a people who can also do magic, but our magic was of no use against them. Their magic was black, strong and overpowering."

Ruth leaned forward staring at her, "You ... you can do magic?" she asked.

Sev nodded.

"You can't?" Roe asked in a surprised voice, looking at Ruth.

Sev continued what she was saying,

"The Darkness swept across our world, destroying ... killing and enslaving our people. They steal people's souls and take them into another world through a gate."

"Or steal their soul's when they're on the other side of the gate," Roe said.

"That triangle thingy we saw in the field!" Ruth said, glancing at Rebecca.

Sev nodded, "Yes, the gate is triangular. We do not know what happens to the people once they enter that other world."

"So ... how did you escape?" Rebecca asked.

"We hid, beneath the castle," Roe said. "We used our magic to cover the entrance to this cavern so that they would not see it."

"But ... we saw it!" Ruth said.

Roe smiled, "That's because I allowed you to see it," he said. "Here, we are hidden. Here, we are safe."

"There's ... a castle above us?" Jimmy asked.

He glanced up at the cavern's ceiling.

"Yes," Sev said. "There is a way up into it. A secret passage. We never go up there, not now. It's too dangerous. Once, it was a castle that was white in colour, it glowed beautifully in the sunlight. Our people lived there, and in surrounding villages ... they were ... happy times. Now, the castle is black, dark and gloomy, filled with evil. The Darkness lives there now."

"So ... how the hell do 'we' come to be here?" Ruth asked. "I ... I thought other worlds were on other planets!"

"Dimensions," Roe said.

He place his head to one side, "Possibly on other planets too," he added thoughtfully.

"One day, we saw the souls of tall people like yourselves being brought into our world through a different gate. The gate had no images and was only covered in darkness. They were transferred to another gate with the image of a different world. The world from where the Darkness comes."

"We believe," Roe said, "that our world is a bridge between different worlds. That is why our world was taken. From here, they could enter different worlds, like yours, directly."

Sev glanced at her husband

"They 'can' enter different worlds directly without passing through 'our' world." she said. "But not physically. In dreams ... nightmares ... or if ... someone contacts them."

Ruth stared at them both, "Wait a minute. Are you saying, that our dreams can be ... controlled by ... by these things? You mean like, nightmares or something?"

Sev nodded, "yes."

"So ... er ... you're basically talking about the ... the Devil, right?" Ruth asked.

Both Jimmy and Rebecca looked at her.

"We know it as the Darkness," Roe said. "Our world was overpowered by it, and our people controlled by it. We thought that ... if other worlds, possibly your world, has the same problem, we could work together and somehow ... defeat it."

"We placed a spell on the dark gate to your world," Sev said. "A small spell that the dark ones would not detect. The spell of communication."

Rebecca stared at her, "You mean ... something that could make us understand each other's language?"

Sev nodded, "If we can communicate, we can work together."

"So ... that's how you can speak English!" Rebecca said.

Roe smiled, "No, that's how you can speak Getriese!"

"Get!" Ruth said, correcting him.

Roe gazed at her questioningly.

"You like 'short' names, right?" Ruth said with a smile, happy to be able to correct him.

It was obvious from Roe's gaze that he didn't like to be corrected.

"Has the invasion of your world started yet?" Sev asked. "Will there be more of you coming through to help us?"

Rebecca looked at them both, then glanced at Jimmy and Ruth sitting beside her.

"We're all there is," Rebecca said, turning back to them. "As for the invasion ... "

Jimmy remembered the nightmarish creature he had seen moving in the darkness through the night when he was a child.

"Maybe it's already started," Jimmy said.

CHAPTER 16

The huge black castle stood on top of a hill overlooking the surrounding land, its spires reaching up towards dark rolling clouds as lightning flashed and thunder boomed overhead.

Inside the castle, Ellie stood in a large hall surrounded by strange looking creatures on either side of her. She was standing in front of four steps that led up to a throne. On the throne sat a tall dark creature called the Darkness. His body was covered in a black cloak, his features hidden beneath a hood. His black and claw-like hands held the sides of the throne tightly.

"This puny creature comes from the other world," he said, his voice deep and menacing as he spoke. The Darkness lifted his right hand upwards and a reddish light appeared, bathing Ellie in its brightness as it shone down around her as if from nowhere. Ellie remained still, staring straight ahead as if she were in some kind of trance.

"She is fair," the Darkness' deep voice said, as he gazed upon Ellie's youthful body. The Darkness studied her extremely pretty face, her blue eyes, her golden hair that hung in locks past her shoulders.

"Such beauty," the Darkness said, studying her carefully, "and so innocent."

The Darkness waved his hand and suddenly Ellie's clothes disappeared. Every creature in the hall gazed upon Ellie's naked body with interest. The tall dark creature on the throne moved his hand again and Ellie turned around, bathed in the light, as if displaying fashionable clothes to the surrounding crowd. When she was once again facing the throne, the Darkness grunted, then waved his hand again. This time, clothes appeared on Ellie's body. The clothes were different. Ellie was now wearing a short black-lace thigh length dress with black knee-high boots.

"Better!" the Darkness said, appraisingly.

The light surrounding Ellie disappeared.

"Go now, and find your friends!" the Darkness said.

Ellie turned, her eyes still glazed as if she were hypnotized, and walked back along the hall towards two large open doors at the end. A bald-headed creature with piercing red eyes, red skin and wearing a black cloak approached the tall dark creature on the throne from the side.

"Are you sure she will be able to find them master?" the red-skinned creature asked.

"The connection with her friends is strong," the Darkness said. "Do you not feel that, Krawl?"

Krawl bowed his head, "Sadly, I do not possess the strength of your powers master," he said.

"Sadly?" the Darkness said, looking at him. "If you did, you would wish my throne perhaps?"

Krawl bowed down even further, "No! No master! ... No! ... I ... I do not mean ...!"

The tall dark creature opened his hand towards him. Suddenly, Krawl felt something around his throat strangling him. His body rose up off the floor as if he were now weightless. He gasped, choking as the invisible grip on his throat squeezed harder. Krawl hung suspended in mid-air, his legs kicking beneath him.

The Darkness lowered his hand and watched as Krawl fell back down and lay gasping and grasping at his throat as he tried to breathe. Every creature, lined up on both sides of the hall, stared up at the scene fearfully.

"Go!" the Darkness ordered, gazing down at Krawl who now knelt on the floor beside him still trying to breathe normally.

"Go follow her! When she finds them, bring them back here!"

Krawl managed to get back up onto his feet. He nodded, keeping his head bowed, "Yes ... yes master!" he managed to say, still grasping at his throat. "Of ... of course master!"

Then he turned, and stumbling, went down the steps and dashed across the hall, running after Ellie who had now disappeared through the huge open doors at the far end. The Darkness watched him go and growled menacingly as the other creatures standing in the hall stared up at him fearfully.

CHAPTER 17

Rebecca walked around the cavern beside Sev away from the others.

"So ... are we stuck here now?" she asked.

Small groups of surrounding little people stared up at her curiously as she passed them.

"If you can get back to the black gate," Sev said, "without being captured, I think you can get back to your world."

"Can you help us?" Rebecca asked. "Show us how to get back to the gate without getting caught?"

Sev stopped walking and looked up at her.

"The invasion into your world has begun," she said. "When you return, you may find that your world is completely different, governed by the Darkness, as is ours."

"Then ... there is no hope?" Rebecca asked. "It's like going from the frying pan back into the fire?"

Sev touched Rebecca's arm, "There may be a way," she said. "The Darkness has a weakness."

Rebecca stared down at her.

"What is it?" she asked.

Sev gazed up at her for a moment, then shook her head, "That, we don't know. But we 'do' know it exists, however, we have yet to find it. Would you ... be willing to stay and help us? Help us rid this world of the Darkness? You see, if there is no Darkness in our world, there can be no bridge to your own."

"But ... you said the invasion into our world has already begun," Rebecca said.

Sev nodded, "True. But if we can find a way to rid the Darkness from our world, you can go back and use the same way to rid the Darkness from yours."

Rebecca stared at her thoughtfully.

"And ... what if we can't?"

Sev continued gazing up at her for a moment, "We must try," she said finally.

Rebecca hesitated, then she nodded, "Okay," she said. "Tell me what we can do."

*

Krawl followed from a distance as Ellie walked across the wide castle courtyard towards the castle gate. Various strange looking creatures stared at her as she passed. Ellie's eyes were open wide as if she were staring at something directly in front of her. As she approached the gate, the gate rose as if by itself to allow her to pass through it. Even though it was around mid-day, the overhead sky was dark with black rolling clouds. A wind rose up to greet her as she stepped outside the gate and stopped walking. She surveyed the landscape beneath her from the hilltop on which the castle stood. The land spread out beneath her like a sea of emerald green towards the ocean and the waves crashing up onto the beach. Had she been in her true state of mind, she would have felt that the view from the castle was beautiful with only the black rolling clouds above to mar its beauty. But Ellie was not in her true state of mind as she gazed coldly down at the scenery below her, her face completely expressionless. Abruptly, she turned to the left and started to make her way down the hill.

*

As Sev and Rebecca returned to the others and sat down once again on the flat stone, Roe suddenly sat upright. He raised his hand and gazed thoughtfully in front of him.

"Someone comes!" he said.

The others sitting nearby looked at him.

"She comes!" Roe continued, his eyes widening as he spoke. "She will be here soon!"

"Who?" Jimmy asked, looking at him. "Who is coming?"

"A friend who is not a friend!" Roe said, still staring into the distance as if he were watching something that he could see on the other side of the cavern.

Sev glanced at Rebecca, "We must all go!" she said. "We will take the escape passage!"

Tol stood up staring at her angrily.

"This is their fault!" he shouted, pointing at Rebecca, Jimmy and Ruth who were standing up behind Sev.

"We were safe! Well hidden! Until they arrived!"

Sev stared at him.

"We were never safe Tol! Never!" Sev said. "This day had to come and you know it!"

Tol sneered bitterly as he stared back at her, then turned and shouted, "Everyone! Go!"

Sev looked at her husband, "Roe, go with them! I will take our friends to the secret passage, the one that leads up into the castle!"

Roe gazed at her, his mouth opening in amazement, "Are you serious?" he asked. "It is too dangerous ... !"

"Go!" Sev said. "Before it is too late! This must be done!"

Roe shook his head, "I will take them ... "

"No!" Sev approached her husband and placed her arms around him.

"You must protect our people," she said. "You can protect them more than I can, you know this to be true!"

Roe hesitated, gazing into Sev's eyes for a moment, then he leaned forward and hugged her tightly

"You be careful!" he said.

Sev smiled and nodded, "I will see you at the other hiding place," she said. "Now, go!"

She watched as Roe ran to join the other people who were running across the cavern towards an escape passage.

"Where are we going?" Ruth asked, turning to Rebecca.

"Us?" Rebecca said, looking at both Ruth and Jimmy. "I guess we're going to try to save their world!"

CHAPTER 18

Ellie was now standing at the base of the hill staring at the rocky wall in front of her.

Krawl, who had been watching her from a distance, slowly moved down the hill and stood behind her. He looked at the wall which Ellie was staring at and saw nothing. Ellie remained still as if she were frozen in place.

"What is it?" Krawl asked. "What do you see?"

But Ellie said nothing and merely remained standing still and staring at the wall of rock facing her. Krawl stared at the rock's surface trying to see what it was that Ellie was staring at. After a moment, he moved closer, then closer still. Something strange seemed to shimmer in front of him bending the light, making the rock's surface go slightly out of focus to his eyes, and as he stepped forward, he felt something. It was as if he had entered a bubble of some sort, like he was going through an invisible wall made of a substance that he couldn't describe.

And then he saw it. The rock's entrance to the passage leading to the large cavern suddenly appeared before him. He now realized what it was he had walked through. Someone had placed a magical spell over the rock's entrance to conceal it. The little people, he thought. So, not only had he found Ellie's friends, but he had also found the little people's hiding place. He smiled, thinking how pleased the master would be. When he turned to look back at Ellie, he saw that she was already beside him. She was standing motionless again, staring at the passage which led inside from the rock's entrance. Suddenly, she moved forward, starting to walk along the passage in front of him. Krawl was amazed to see rocks and stones light up on either side of the passage as she went. He watched her go for a moment, then he followed after her. If he could capture them himself, he thought, the reward would be great.

Krawl's smile widened with this thought as he followed behind Ellie through the passage.

*

Ruth turned to look back at Rebecca as they made their way up an old winding staircase made of stone.

"Would you mind telling me where we're going?" she asked.

"Yes," Jimmy said, glancing back at Rebecca. "You were talking a long time with Sev. What did she tell you?"

"They want us to help them," Rebecca answered.

"Us?" Ruth almost shouted. "How can 'we' help them? They're the ones with the magical powers, not us!"

"It's because of their magical powers that they can easily be detected," Rebecca said. "The moment they step outside of some kind of protective magical shield, the one they used to hide the cavern for example, they run the risk of being found."

"Rue was outside!" Ruth pointed out.

"But only for a short period," Rebecca said. "He felt our presence. He ran the risk to meet us and bring us to safety."

"But ... Ruth is right, they have magic, and we don't!" Jimmy said, looking back at Rebecca as they made their way up the dimly-lit and narrow staircase.

"But their magic is not so strong," Rebecca said. "They can't fight the Darkness."

"And we can?" Ruth asked, looking back at her.

"Maybe," Rebecca said. "We have no magic, they can't detect us, and the Darkness has a weakness, we just need to find it."

"You mean ... no one knows what that weakness is?" Ruth asked.

Rebecca shook her head, "No, not yet. That's why we're going up into the castle, to find it."

"Not yet?" Ruth repeated. "Are you kidding me? We're going up into a castle filled with dark I don't know what, to find a weakness we don't even know exists?"

"It exists," Rebecca said. "We just have to find it!"

"Well, forgive me if I take a break to fill out my will and testament before we go any further!" Ruth said bitterly. "Because I'm really sure we're not going to come out of this alive!"

"They helped us," Rebecca said. "It's only right that we should try to help them."

Rebecca looked at Jimmy as he mounted the staircase in front of her, "How do you feel about this?" she asked.

"I ... I've always been afraid of the dark," Jimmy said, "and I guess it ... it's time to face my fears."

"Hey, wait a minute!" Ruth stopped and turned to face Rebecca. "If these small people can't be detected in their protective shield, and we can't be detected because we have no magical powers, how the hell did they find the cavern?"

Rebecca looked back at her, "Roe said that is was through a friend who is not a friend, but I don't know what he means."

Ruth nodded, "Great!" she said sarcastically, then turned to continue up the stairs.

"Shhhh!" Sev said, from further up the staircase in front of them. "We are approaching the entrance into the castle!" she whispered.

"Oh great!" Ruth muttered under her breath. "I've always wanted to meet the Devil!"

They reached the top of the twisting staircase and Sev searched along the wall to the right with her hand in the semi-darkness under the dim glow of the wall-stones. She found what she was looking for and they heard something 'click'. Part of the wall in front of them made a grating sound as it started to slide open.

"Wow! A secret opening!" Ruth exclaimed.

Sev turned to her, "Shhhh!" she said, placing a finger to her lips. "These walls have ears," she whispered. "You must be quiet."

They stepped through the opening into a large and dusty room filled with tables, chairs, various other pieces of furniture and bookcases with old and dusty books on the shelves.

"This was once a library," Sev whispered, as they made their way across the large room to a door on the other side. Sev opened the door slightly, the door creaking in the silence, and looked out.

"The corridor is empty," she whispered back to them.

Sev turned to Rebecca, "I can go no further," she said. "The Darkness will feel my presence."

"Hey, I have a question about that!" Ruth whispered. "How come Roe could feel our presence, but this Darkness couldn't?"

Rebecca looked at her, "Ruth, we don't have time ... "

"Hey!" Ruth whispered, turning to her. "It's a good question!"

Sev looked at her, "Roe is special," she whispered. "He can feel things others can't." She turned to Rebecca, "Remember what I have told you.

The Darkness keeps one room always locked, it must be so for a reason. The room once used to be the King's chamber, it is near the Great Hall."

"The King?" Jimmy whispered , staring at her. "And where's the King?"

Sev lowered her head sadly, "The King is dead," she whispered, shaking her head. She looked back up at them, "Be careful," Sev said. "If any creatures see you, they will alert the Darkness and you will be captured. They may not kill you ... straight away. Possibly ... torture you first ... for amusement."

Ruth's eyes widened, "Great!" she whispered, staring at Sev. "Anymore nice surprises?"

Rebecca shot Ruth a glance.

"You know where to go?" Sev asked Rebecca.

Rebecca nodded, "I'll just follow your directions."

Sev smiled, then reached up and clasped Rebecca's hands tightly, "Good luck!" she whispered.

Sev turned, looked at both Jimmy and Ruth, then moved past them and went back across the old and dusty library towards the secret opening in the wall.

"So, what do we do now?" Ruth asked, as they watched the secret wall-opening close behind Sev.

"We must find the King's chamber," Rebecca said.

She turned and glanced out through the door into the corridor outside.

The corridor was dimly lit with torches burning here and there fixed to the walls.

"Do you know where to go?" Jimmy asked.

Rebecca nodded, "Sev says it's to the right, along the corridor, turn left, and then it's in the next corridor at the far end."

Jimmy moved forward beside Rebecca to glance out into the corridor.

"Er ... if this is going to be dangerous," Ruth said behind them, "I think I'll stay here."

Rebecca turned to look at her.

"Okay then, you can stay here by yourself."

Both Rebecca and Jimmy stepped out into the corridor closing the door behind them. Ruth remained still looking at the closed door. She turned, glanced around at the dusty and dimly-lit library and felt a chill go through her.

"Oh well!" she muttered to herself, suddenly regretting the idea of staying by herself. She turned back to the door and opened it.

"Hey guys!" she whispered, stepping out into the corridor. "I'm coming with you!"

Both Rebecca and Jimmy turned to look back at her. Rebecca smiled, then turned back to concentrate on the corridor ahead of them. They moved slowly, silently, listening carefully for any sounds as they went. After a moment, they reached the end of the corridor and turned left into the next corridor which was also dimly-lit. They advanced along it slowly, hearing no noise, no sound at all until they came to another corridor, and then they saw the large doors to the king's chamber up ahead of them.

"I really don't like this!" Ruth whispered to herself, glancing around at the corridor with wide eyes.

"Shhhh!" Rebecca said, turning to her.

"Sorry!" Ruth whispered back to her defensively, with a slight pout on her face.

They reached the King's chamber and saw that they were now standing in front of two huge wooden doors.

"What if we can't open it?" Ruth whispered.

Rebecca glanced back at her.

"What ... what if this Darkness is inside?" Ruth continued.

Rebecca turned to face her, "Must you always be so pessimistic?" she asked.

"If it means being a 'live' pessimistic, yes!" Ruth whispered back.

Rebecca shook her head, then turned back to the doors. Jimmy had already moved forward and was turning a large metal ring in the door which he assumed was a handle. Something 'clicked' and the door slowly opened.

"Er ... didn't Sev say that it should be locked?" Ruth said, staring at the now open door with wide fear-filled eyes.

"Never look a gift horse in the mouth," Rebecca said, glancing at her.

"Okay," Ruth said, nodding. "But do you mind if I worry about it a little?"

Jimmy pushed the door further open and stepped inside cautiously.

If the room had once been the King's chamber, then it had been changed dramatically. Although there was a small light inside, everything was coloured in black. The walls, the floor, the high ceiling, even the surrounding furniture, some of which looked very strange, were all in black. Strangely enough for a King's chamber, there was no sign of a bed, only a large mass of black strange-looking substance which lay in a rectangular shaped hole in the floor. Ruth Followed Jimmy and Rebecca into the chamber and closed the door behind her. She gazed around the room feeling a tingling sensation of fear creeping up her spine.

"What the hell is this?" she said, gazing around at the totally black room.

She looked across at the window opposite and saw nothing outside beneath the dark storm clouds.

"What are we looking for?" Jimmy asked, turning back towards Rebecca.

Rebecca stared down at the strange, almost liquid-like black substance in the rectangular hole, "I don't know," she said. "Sev said that the Darkness has a weakness, she thinks that we can find out what it is in this room."

"She thinks?" Ruth said. "Nice!" she shivered. "I think we should go!"

Both Rebecca and Jimmy walked around the room searching for anything unusual.

"But ... then," Ruth continued. "I ... I guess no one really cares what I think, right?" she said, now standing in the middle of the black room and glancing around fearfully.

"The Darkness must have a weakness," Rebecca said.

"Sure," Ruth said, looking around. "I guess everybody does, right? Alcohol, drugs, porn mags ..."

"Hey!" she cried out, after a moment, "I've got it!"

Both Rebecca and Jimmy turned to look at her.

"He has a strong aversion to the colour white!" she said.

Rebecca narrowed her eyes as she stared at her.

Ruth shrugged as she looked back at her friend, "What?" she asked defensively.

Jimmy noticed something in one corner of the room, almost completely obscured in the dim light.

"Hey!" he called. "Over here! There's a ... a big chest here!"

Rebecca ran over to him. Together, they knelt down staring at it.

"It's huge!" Rebecca said, reaching out a hand to touch the surface of the huge black chest.

She ran her hand over it, "It has markings on it," she said.

Jimmy leaned forward trying to make out the markings.

"They're strange," he said. "Never ... seen markings like that before."

Rebecca glanced at him, "Whatever we're looking for, it has to be inside this," she said. She took a deep breath, "Are you ready?" she asked.

Jimmy glanced at her, then nodded. They both placed their hands on top of the chest to open it.

Suddenly, from behind them, Ruth screamed.

CHAPTER 19

Both Rebecca and Jimmy jerked round as Ruth's scream filled the room.

"What is it?" Rebecca asked.

Ruth, who was still standing in the centre of the black room, was staring at the wall on the left with wide fear-filled eyes. She raised her hand shakily and pointed towards it.

"The ... the ... there!" she managed to say with a trembling voice.

Both Rebecca and Jimmy looked towards the wall.

"It ...it's an eye!" Ruth said in amazement.

Both Rebecca and Jimmy stared at the eye.

It was large, much larger than a normal eye. It was staring directly at them from the wall, as if it were part of the wall, imbedded in it. The eye blinked. Ruth let out another scream and jerked back away from it. Suddenly, other eyes appeared in the black wall staring at them, and then others, until the whole wall seemed to be covered with them.

"Oh my God!" Ruth gasped, raising her hands to her mouth and stepping further back away from the wall now filled with staring eyes. As she took one more step back, she fell. Ruth screamed out loudly as she fell into the large rectangular hole filled with a soft liquid-like black substance that seemed to absorb her like quicksand as she went into it.

"Ruth!" Rebecca cried out, moving quickly towards the hole.

Jimmy joined her and they both reached forward from the side of the hole to grab Ruth as she disappeared beneath the black liquid-like surface. They both reached down, unable to see her, searching for her with their hands in the sticky black substance.

"Ruth!" Rebecca cried out again as they searched desperately for her.

Jimmy found her arm and began to pull her up. As he pulled her to the surface Rebecca helped him to pull her out. Together, they pulled her out of the hole and onto the floor. Ruth lay still, gasping for breath and surprisingly wasn't covered in the strange black substance which seemed to slip away from her as she was pulled out.

"Th ... thank you!" she gasped, turning over and coughing as she spoke.

Rebecca looked back up at the eyes on the wall. They were all staring down at them.

Jimmy sighed with relief, glancing down at Ruth as she continued to cough on the floor, then he stood up went back over to the chest.

"It ... it must've known we were here!" he said. "We ... we have to be fast!"

Rebecca turned her eyes away from the wall and went over to join him, "Right!" she agreed.

They both looked down at the huge black chest in front of them.

Jimmy glanced at her, "Let's do it!" he said.

Rebecca nodded, and then together, they lifted the lid of the chest.

Rebecca gasped as she gazed down inside.

Something was moving inside the chest in front of them. It was turning, swirling, spinning.

They both stared down at what seemed to be miniature storm inside the centre of the chest with dark clouds turning and swirling fast in a strong wind. Occasionally, there were bursts of light as if caused by lightning followed by a deep booming sound of thunder.

"What the hell ... ?" Rebecca said, as both she and Jimmy stared down at the mini-storm inside the chest in complete amazement.

"Hell!" Rebecca exclaimed, looking across at Jimmy. "What do we do now?"

Suddenly, the door behind them opened.

CHAPTER 20

Jimmy opened his eyes.

He felt cold and stiff. As he moved he saw that he was lying on a cold stone floor. He grunted, leaning up slowly and looked around. He saw that he was in a large and dimly-lit chamber. Various instruments of torture hung from the walls or were piled together in different parts of the chamber. He heard someone gasp and quickly turned to see Rebecca lying beside him.

"Rebecca!" he cried, moving closer to her.

Slowly, Rebecca opened her eyes and saw him. She leaned up, raising her hand to her head feeling a slight dizziness.

"Where are we?" she asked, gazing quickly around the dimly-lit chamber. "What happened?"

"I ... I don't know," Jimmy said, trying to remember. "The ... the door opened ... and then ... "

"Total blackness," Rebecca said, finishing Jimmy's sentence for him. "My head's spinning," she said. "Did you ... did you see who came in?"

Jimmy shook his head, staring at the instruments of torture which surrounded them, "No. I ... I must've blacked out, like you."

Rebecca looked around, "Where's Ruth?" she asked.

Jimmy also looked around.

"I ... I don't know," he answered..

Rebecca stood up, still holding her head, "We ... we have to find her!" she said.

Jimmy stood up beside her, "I'll try the door."

He crossed the chamber to the large wooden door and tried to open it.

"It's locked," he said.

Rebecca went over to join him and also tried to open it.

"Completely locked," she said, giving up.

She turned to look at the dimly-lit chamber.

"What is this place?" she asked.

"It looks like some kind of ... torture chamber," Jimmy said, gazing round.

Rebecca stared at the various instruments of torture in the chamber and shivered involuntarily.

"Do ... do you think they're going to torture us?" Rebecca asked.

"I hope not," Jimmy said.

"I hope not too!" Rebecca said. "I have a low pain resistance level!"

She glanced back at the various instruments of torture, her eyes lingering on the racks which were used to bound people in a bent over position. She thought about being bound on them helplessly and waiting, as someone ... or something, prepared to torture her. The feeling scared her. She remained staring at the many kinds of racks, and on each one she imagined being bound in a different position, completely and utterly helpless. She looked at a standing wooden cross and imagined being bound spread-eagled to it. She shivered again.

She turned to look at Jimmy, "We have to get out of here!" she said.

Jimmy nodded, "I know," he said. "But how?"

Rebecca glanced once more around the chamber, "Maybe ... maybe we can find something we can use to try to open the door," she said. "Help me search."

Jimmy nodded again and went over to the other end of the chamber to look for anything they could use to open the door.

*

Ruth stood in the Great Hall. She stared around her with wide eyes filled with fear as her whole body trembled uncontrollably. She was standing in front of three steps leading up to a throne. Standing around her in the hall and staring at her curiously was an assortment of strange nightmarish looking creatures. She had no idea how she got there, and without either Rebecca or Jimmy to be with her she felt terribly alone, frightened, and very, very vulnerable. A door opened to her right and she jerked towards the sound with a frightened gasp. A tall dark cloaked and hooded creature seemed to glide across the floor and up towards the throne, followed by other strange and nightmarish looking creatures who entered the hall, each of them staring at her as they entered. Ruth gazed down, afraid to look at them, trying to stop the trembling in her body but unable to. She was aware that her fear of them was obvious. She remained standing in place, trembling in fear with her head bowed as the tall dark creature moved across above her sat down in the throne.

"This is the tall one master," a creature with red skin said to the tall dark creature now sitting on the throne.

"And the others Krawl?" the Darkness, Krawl referred to as 'master', said, in deep menacing tones.

Krawl smiled, with his head bowed towards his master, "I have left them in the torture chamber, master," he said. "They are awaiting your personal enjoyment. I thought you might like some entertainment with them."

"Yessss … " the Darkness said, studying Ruth carefully, noticing her fear-filled eyes and her trembling body.

The Darkness reached out a hand down towards her.

"Perfect! Her fear is so strong!" he said. "I could almost touch it!"

"I am pleased you like her master," Krawl said, keeping his head bowed humbly.

"And what of the fair beauty?" the Darkness asked.

Krawl immediately turned and clapped his hands and two creatures brought Ellie into the hall between them.

"Ellie!" Ruth cried out in shock as she glanced up and saw her friend enter the hall. Ruth tried to move forwards towards her but felt that she couldn't. She seemed to be stuck, as if her feet couldn't move, as if somehow they were glued to the floor.

"Ellie!" Ruth cried out again. "Ellie!"

But Ellie remained still, staring in front of her as if she were in some kind of trance.

The Darkness turned to Krawl who was standing beside the throne, "Bring the rack!" he ordered.

Once again Krawl clapped his hands and two other creatures entered wheeling a vertical rack towards where Ruth was standing, literally rooted to the spot.

"Bind her!" the Darkness ordered.

The two creatures grabbed Ruth's arms. Ruth screamed as they pulled her onto the vertical rack and began binding her wrists and ankles to its four corners. Ruth struggled as they bound her, but the creatures were too strong for her. When they had finished they stepped away. The Darkness gazed down at Ruth and grinned. Ruth was now bound spread-eagled to the vertical rack. He watched as she pulled at her bonds trying to free herself, but she was now bound firmly in place. Finally she gave up trying, realizing that she was bound completely helpless, and began to whimper as her body trembled uncontrollably. Suddenly, the Darkness leaned forward in his throne and waved his hand. Ruth screamed and began pulling frantically at her bonds once more, her face turning bright red in embarrassment as her clothes disappeared. Each of the creatures stared at her now naked body with interest. Ruth began to sob and beg, too afraid to even imagine what terrible things they were going to do, or could do to her, and then the Darkness waved his hand again and the next instant a long black gown appeared on her body. The Darkness grunted as if displeased and then waved his hand again. Once again, her body was clothed in something different, this time she was wearing a short black leather tunic. Ruth gazed down in amazement at the black tunic which she was now wearing. The Darkness grunted again in displeasure, then once again waved his hand. This time, a white and very short ancient-looking Greek-styled dress adorned Ruth's body. Ruth stared down at it in total disbelief.

The Darkness grunted in satisfaction, then turned to Krawl, "Bring the hands!" he ordered. He then sat back in the throne to watch. Two creatures carrying two large wooden boxes entered the hall. Ruth watched as they came over and placed the boxes on the floor in front of her. Ruth stared down at the boxes with wide fear-filled eyes wondering what was inside, and then the creatures opened them. What came out of them made Ruth gasp in horror. At least ten severed hands crawled out of each box. They moved slowly across the floor towards her, using their fingers and crawling as if they were spiders moving towards their prey.

Ruth screamed!

She pulled frantically at her bonds, continuing to scream as the hands reached her feet and then began climbing up her legs. Ruth's eyes opened wider in fear as she screamed and cried and pulled at the bonds, holding her firmly bound, with all her might. The hands reached her thighs and continued crawling upwards. Four of them disappeared beneath the short white Greek-styled dress while the others continued moving slowly up and over her body. Ruth threw her head back and screamed at the top of her lungs as she writhed frantically in her bonds. Suddenly, her screams were stifled as one hand appeared on her shoulder and crawled over to cover her mouth tightly in its grasp. Ruth's eyes bulged, her screams were now muffled as the hands crawled all over her body forcing her to writhe and jerk and buck helplessly in her bonds as a deep sounding laughter could be heard echoing around the walls of the large hall.

CHAPTER 21

Jimmy beat at the locked door with a heavy metal clamp used for torturing various parts of the body. After a moment, he stopped beating at the door and rested against it breathing heavily.

"It's useless!" he said, glancing back at Rebecca who was standing behind him.

"Try again," Rebecca said. "It's the only way. It's all we've got!"

Jimmy sighed, "Okay," he said, picking up the heavy torturing device once more.

Jimmy hit the door with it again, and then again, and again. Suddenly, on his fourth renewed attempt, he heard something break. Jimmy dropped the device to the floor and reached forward to the door. He pushed it, and the door moved slowly forward, creaking on its hinges as it went.

Rebecca grinned behind him, "Well done!" she said, moving forward to the door.

She pushed the door open wider and peeked out. The corridor looked dark, only a few torches were burning in the fixtures on the walls.

"I guess this must be the basement," she whispered back to Jimmy. "Dungeons and torture chambers are usually in basements."

"We have to find your friend Ruth," Jimmy whispered. He looked along the corridor at the heavy wooden doors which lined both sides of it. "Do you think she's in one of these dungeons?" he asked.

"Maybe," Rebecca whispered. "But I don't see why they would split us up. You go to the right, I'll go to the left. We'll check every dungeon."

"Jimmy nodded, "Right."

They moved out and into the corridor, each going separate ways and moving as fast as they could, checking each dungeon as they went. All of the dungeons were unlocked and empty, except one. Rebecca came to the last dungeon on her side of the corridor and found that it was locked.

"Ruth?" she called out, looking at the locked door in front of her. "Ruth! Are you in there? ... Ruth?"

Jimmy came running back to join her.

"No one in the other dungeons," he said.

"This one's locked," Rebecca said, glancing at him. "Ruth!" she called out again. "Ruth, are you in there?"

On the other side of the door they heard a shuffling noise, and then a voice.

"Who is it?" the voice said.

The voice was a man's.

Rebecca looked at Jimmy, then back at the locked door, "We're friends," Rebecca said. "Don't worry! We'll get you out of there! We can break the lock!"

"The keys!" the man's voice said. "The keys are hung on a hook next to the door at the end of the corridor!"

Both Rebecca and Jimmy looked towards the door at the end of the corridor and saw the keys glinting in the light from a nearby burning torch hanging on the wall.

"I'll get them!" Jimmy said.

He ran along the corridor to get them while Rebecca moved closer to the dungeon door.

"Who are you?" she asked.

There was a momentary silence, and then the voice spoke.

"I am the King," the voice said.

Rebecca leaned back and stared at the door in surprise. Jimmy came running back with a set of keys attached to a large ring.

"We've got the keys!" Rebecca said.

Jimmy placed the first one in the lock but it didn't open the door. He tried another, and another, and then, on the fourth key, he heard the a 'click' in the lock.

Rebecca pushed the door open. Inside, in the dim light, she saw a small dark cell with nothing but straw on the floor. Standing to one side was a short man. His hair and beard were white and as he stepped out of the dungeon they saw that his eyes were tired as if he had not slept for a very long time. His clothes, probably once regal looking, now looked old and ragged.

"Who are you?" he asked, looking up at them both.

"We're friends," Rebecca said.

"Yes, you already said that," the king said.

"The Darkness has our friend," Jimmy said.

"Have you seen her?" Rebecca asked. "A tall girl with brown hair."

The King stared at them both.

"If The darkness has your friend, then she will be in the Great Hall. It is where they have their ... entertainment."

Rebecca stared back at him, "Enter ... entertainment?" she repeated, shocked by the word.

The King nodded, "Yes."

"What ... what kind of ... ?"

"Can you take us there?" Jimmy asked.

The king nodded, "But it will do you no good. If they have your friend in the Great Hall, you will not be able to help her. Perhaps it is wise that you escape with me."

Rebecca shook her head, "I'm not leaving her!"

"Your ... your majesty," Jimmy said.

The King looked at him. He stood a little more erect at the sound of his title.

"What do you know about the chest in your chamber? It belongs to the Darkness, is that right?"

The King remained still, staring at him for a moment, then he nodded, "Yes,' he said.

"How ... how is it his weakness?" Jimmy asked.

Rebecca glanced at Jimmy, "We don't have time for this! We have to find Ruth!"

Jimmy looked back at her.

"If ... if the Darkness isn't destroyed, then no one is safe ... ever!"

He turned back to the King, "How is it his weakness?" he asked.

"Inside," the King said, "there is a storm. The Darkness brings the storm to all worlds he wishes to conquer."

He glanced down sadly, "As he did mine. It is said, that if the storm were to stop, his powers would also stop, his control over others ... "

"So, how do you stop the storm?" Jimmy asked. "Must we ... must we break the chest?"

The King shook his head.

"No! You must never break it! If you did, the storm would be uncontrollable!"

"So, what do we do?" Rebecca asked. "How can you stop a storm?"

The King was silent for a moment glancing down thoughtfully, then he spoke.

"With a key," he said.

"A key?" Jimmy repeated.

"It is said that if a certain key is placed in the lock of the box and turned, it will lock the storm inside, containing it, forbidding it from getting out."

Both Jimmy and Rebecca glanced at each other.

"And where is this key?" Rebecca asked, looking back at the King.

"The Darkness has it," the King said. "It hangs around his neck. No one can take it ... no one! He's too ... powerful!"

Rebecca looked at Jimmy, "If he has Ruth in the Great Hall, then they are both there, Ruth and the key!"

Jimmy nodded, then looked at the King.

"Take us to the Great Hall," he said.

CHAPTER 22

"This is a secret passage," the King said, holding a burning torch up high and glancing back at both Rebecca and Jimmy who were following behind him. "Only a few people know about it. It leads to a secret opening in the Great Hall."

They turned a bend in the passage and continued along it until they came to what looked like a dead end.

"It doesn't lead anywhere!" Rebecca said, looking at the wall now in front of them.

The King turned and raised his finger for them to be quiet.

"Shhhh! The Great Hall lies beyond this door," he whispered. "You must be quiet."

He handed Jimmy the burning torch, then turned and felt alongside the wall with his fingers. After a few moments, he found what he was looking for and pressed against the wall. Both Rebecca and Jimmy watched in amazement as the wall opened slightly. The King pushed it forward just enough so that he could look into the Great Hall. Rebecca and

Jimmy moved up behind him to gaze through the gap. What they saw made them gasp. A crowd of strange looking creatures were gathered around the hall. They saw an imposing figure dressed completely in black with a hood covering his features sitting on a throne. This, they thought, was obviously the Darkness. They saw Ellie standing to one side and gasped once again in Surprise.

"Ellie!" Rebecca said. "How did she get here?"

Jimmy's heart beat faster as he stared at her perfect features and her golden hair. She was standing and staring straight ahead as if she were hypnotized. Beside her was a strange looking red skinned creature.

"Wha ... what's wrong with her?" Jimmy stuttered.

"The Darkness has her in his control," the King answered.

Then they saw what all of the creatures in the hall were staring at. Ruth was bound spread-eagled and upside down on a vertical rack. At least twenty severed hands were crawling across her body, using their fingers as if they were spiders, as if each one had a life of its own. Ruth was jerking and writhing uncontrollably in her bonds, gasping, begging and screaming as the hands played over her helpless and firmly bound body.

"Oh my God!" Rebecca uttered, staring in both shock and disbelief at the scene in front of her.

She turned to the King, "What ...?"

"Magic," the King said. "The Darkness ... he can control everything ... everyone. This is just one way he entertains his creatures. There are worst tortures, believe me! Your friend is lucky she is not being tortured painfully."

"Lucky?" Rebecca repeated, almost shouting the word. "We ... we have to do something! We have to stop this!"

"The key," the King said. "It is the only way!"

Rebecca looked across the Great Hall at the Darkness sitting on the King's throne. She saw the key hanging from a chain around his neck.

"What if we run in ...?" Jimmy started to say.

"You wouldn't get five feet," the King said. "If the creatures don't get you, the Darkness with his powers certainly will."

"We've got to do something!" Rebecca said, feeling helpless as she watched the severed hands crawling all over Ruth's spread-eagled and upturned body.

"Wha ... what can we do?" Jimmy asked, looking at the King.

The King turned to him, then gave a sad smile.

"Wait," he said. "We can only wait, until the time is right."

Suddenly, across the hall, Ruth gave an ear-piercing scream as she bucked uncontrollably, pulling with all her might at the bonds holding her limbs firmly apart.

"I can't!" Rebecca said, staring with tear-filled eyes towards her friend.

"You must," the King said, glancing at her.

He closed the secret entrance to the Great Hall.

"You must," he repeated, turning to look at them both.

CHAPTER 23

Rebecca sat on the floor of the passage wiping the tears from her face. Jimmy sat opposite her looking across at her sadly. The King gazed at them both, then stood up.

"We have waited long enough," he said.

He moved to the secret entrance, touched something in the wall beside it, and then pushed the secret entrance slightly open.

He leaned forward, peering through the gap in the wall. The Great Hall now seemed empty. The creatures were no longer there, neither was the Darkness sitting on the throne, but there was one small sound coming from the hall, the sound of someone crying and sobbing. The King pushed the entrance open further and glanced back at Rebecca and Jimmy.

"Come!" he said.

Both Rebecca and Jimmy stood up and followed the King out through the secret entrance and entered the Great Hall. There, in its centre, they saw Ruth. She was still bound spread-eagled to the vertical rack, but now she was no longer upside down. The short white Greek-looking dress that she had been wearing was now ripped and torn on the floor beside her. There were marks all over her naked body.

"Ruth!" Rebecca called out. Both she and Jimmy ran over to her.

Rebecca stood in front of her, tears once again falling down onto her cheeks.

"R ... Rebecca?" Ruth managed to say weakly as she sobbed. She glanced at Jimmy who was now standing beside Rebecca, and her face immediately went red at the embarrassment of being bound naked and helplessly spread in front of him.

Ruth sobbed and quickly glanced down away from his eyes.

"Help me untie her!" Rebecca said urgently.

Together, they untied the bonds binding her wrists and ankles as quickly as possible and helped her down off the rack. Ruth fell forward into Rebecca's arms sobbing uncontrollably.

"Are you okay?" Rebecca asked, squeezing her friend tightly in her arms. "Are you okay?"

Ruth tried to answer, but couldn't as she continued to sob against Rebecca who continued to hug her tightly.

Rebecca gently pulled back Ruth's head and looked into her face.

"Don't worry, we've got you," she said. "We've got you. We'll get you out of here, okay? ... Okay?"

Suddenly, they heard something like an alarm and shouting outside in the corridor.

"They have discovered our escape!" The King said. "Quickly! Into the passage!"

Jimmy looked at Rebecca, "What about your friend? Ellie?" he asked. "We can't just leave her!"

"No time! No time!" the King called out, heading back across the Great Hall to the secret entrance in the wall.

"Let's get Ruth to safety first!" Rebecca said, looking at Jimmy.

Jimmy shook his head.

"I'm not leaving without her!" he said.

"You're the one who told me getting the key was the most important thing!" Rebecca said.

Jimmy stared at her.

Rebecca was right, he knew that she was right, and yet, he could not stop his heart from pumping wildly when he thought about Ellie. They heard the shouting coming closer in the corridor outside the Great Hall. Someone was coming.

"Come on!" Rebecca said, turning with the sobbing Ruth in her arms to follow the King who was now waiting for them at the secret entrance to the passage.

"Jimmy! Help me with her!" Rebecca called back to him urgently.

Jimmy hesitated.

He glanced towards the two huge closed doors at the end of the Great Hall. The shouts coming from the corridor now sounded as if they were just outside.

"Jimmy!" Rebecca called out, as she struggled to help Ruth cross the hall towards the secret entrance.

Fighting the strength of the feelings he had for Ellie in his heart, he turned, picked up what was left of Ruth's torn Greek styled dress and ran over to Rebecca to help her across the hall with Ruth towards the secret entrance which the King had now already entered.

*

"They have escaped!" Krawl said to the Darkness with his head bowed. There was fear in his voice as he spoke.

The Darkness gazed around the torture chamber, then back at the broken lock on the door.

"Your responsibility!" the Darkness said, turning angrily to Krawl. "Your failure! You find them!"

Another creature entered the torture chamber behind them. He bowed his head in fear as he spoke.

"The King has escaped master!"

The Darkness stared at him. He could feel the creature's fear, see his body trembling.

"Find them!" he bellowed, his deep voice seeming to boom like thunder. "Find them! Or you will feel my wrath!"

The creature immediately turned and disappeared from the chamber.

"I ... I will look for them!" Krawl said nervously. He turned to Ellie, who was standing stiffly beside him, "Come!" he said.

Ellie began to follow him, still in her trance-like state.

"The girl stays!" the Darkness boomed.

Krawl stopped in his tracks. He glanced back at Ellie.

"But ... she ..." Krawl started to say, his voice trembling as he spoke.

"I said she stays!" the Darkness shouted, glaring angrily towards Krawl.

Krawl immediately bowed, "Y ... yes! Of ... of course master! As you wish!" he said stuttering, with a look of fear in his eyes as he spoke.

He quickly turned and left the chamber.

The Darkness watched him leave, then turned his attention to Ellie. Ellie stood staring straight ahead, as still as if she were a statue. The Darkness waved his hand and within seconds Ellie's eyes flickered and she began to move as if she were waking up and coming out of a dream.

"Wh ... where am I?" she said, gazing around.

Then she saw the Darkness standing in front of her, watching her.

Ellie screamed.

She backed away, stumbling over the torture devices scattered about on the torture chamber floor. She glanced down and saw the various devices, and then screamed again. The Darkness approached her, watching her closely.

"Your fear is strong," the Darkness said, as Ellie continued to back away from him across the torture chamber.

"That is good," the Darkness said. "I feel your fear!" he breathed in deeply as if savouring what he felt. "It feels so good!" he said.

The Darkness stopped walking forward and held out his hand, "Let me feed on your fear!" his voice boomed.

Suddenly, Ellie's body rose up off the floor and glided quickly back across the chamber towards him, just as if there were a force pulling her forward towards him like a magnet.

Ellie screamed as the Darkness now reached out and grabbed her. The next moment, a dark red smoke-like substance seemed to exude from her body towards him. The Darkness breathed it in deeply as his hands gripped her tightly in front of him. Ellie continued screaming and writhing trying to free herself from his grip. The Darkness gasped in pleasure as if he were drinking a sweet nectar.

"Ahh, fear!" his voice boomed. "So sweet! So powerful!"

He grinned, staring into Ellie's wide and fear-filled eyes.

"After … we will play a game!" he said, his deep voice seeming to boom loudly and echo around the chamber. "Or rather … my creatures will play … with you!"

Suddenly, three strange and grotesquely looking creatures came into the torture chamber and gazed across at her. Ellie stared at them in terror as she continued to scream and writhe helplessly in the strong grip the Darkness had on her. Her screams filled the entire chamber, but there was no one to hear, no one to help her, as the Darkness began to laugh at her futile attempts to escape his grip.

CHAPTER 24

The thought of Ellie kept going through Jimmy's mind as he followed the King and Rebecca, who was still helping Ruth along the secret passage. They entered a second passage to the right and continued along it. The passage seemed to slant downwards as they walked and after a moment grew steeper as it continued to go down. Rebecca almost slipped and Jimmy rushed forward to help her with Ruth. After some time they finally came to the end of the passage as they turned a corner. The King immediately went to the rock wall in front of them and touched something on its side. There was a rumbling sound and the rock wall began sliding to the left. They stepped forward out of the darkened passage and into the pouring rain outside. The King turned and closed the wall entrance to the secret passage behind them. As they came away from the rock wall and started walking towards the trees, Jimmy glanced back and saw that they were now at the bottom of the hill under the castle. Lightning flashed and thunder boomed across the dark sky above them. The black castle rose up from the hilltop as if it were a brooding evil monster, as dark clouds rolled around it almost seeming to embrace it.

"Where are we?" Rebecca called to the King above the booming noise of the thunder as she helped Ruth on towards the trees.

"We are entering the forest at the bottom of the castle," the King called out. "This way! Quickly!"

The King was gesturing towards the trees on the left. Jimmy hesitated, staring back up at the castle and thinking of Ellie.

"Come!" the King called urgently, glancing back at him. "You cannot help her now! You must save yourself!"

Jimmy hesitated a moment longer, then reluctantly turned and began to follow the others through the forest.

*

Rain poured down from the dark sky as six horsemen riding black horses left the castle riding along the road towards the forest. Each of them was dressed in black. Krawl followed behind them on a grey horse. The words of his master echoed in his mind, "Find them!" his voice had boomed menacingly. "Find them or you will feel my wrath!"

Krawl lowered his head meekly, trying to still his trembling hands as he rode. He knew he did not need the girl to find them, he knew that the horsemen could find them due to the magical 'imprint' that the Darkness had placed upon the back of the King's head without his knowledge. He knew that it was not through necessity that he wanted the girl to be with him to aid in their search, but it was rather a desire, a desire he felt for her. After he had left the torture chamber, he had feared what the master would do to her. He realized that his desire for her was great. He had never seen a creature so fair, so beautiful. He thought of her being bound to a vertical rack, as her tall friend had been, thought of her having her clothes taken from her as she stared at the Darkness with wide fear-filled eyes and sobbing uncontrollably. He thought of his master, and of the other creatures the master favoured, approaching her. Krawl closed his eyes tightly, trying to erase the image from his mind. After he had left the torture chamber, he had softly closed the door and had turned away. He had watched the master's favoured creatures approaching the chamber and had waited, listening as they had entered. As he heard Ellie's screams, he had clenched his hands tightly into fists wishing that he could go to her, be with her, then he had turned and walked quickly along the corridor away from the torture chamber, hearing Ellie's screams fading behind him as he went. He feared that her beauty, that her fairness would be taken from her. Krawl continued to think about her as he rode in the rain behind the six horsemen, hoping that when he returned, she would still be as beautiful and as fair as when he had first seen her. He tried to push her out of his mind, and then spurred his horse on with only one thought in his mind, find the others! For if he did not, he knew that it would be he who would be tortured next, and his torture would probably be far, far worse.

*

The King reached a group of rocks nearby a clearing in the woods and stopped.

"What are we stopping for?" Rebecca asked from behind him.

Ruth, who was being held up between Rebecca and Jimmy, groaned. She was barely conscious, and seemed to be coming on with some kind of fever.

"It is here!" the King said, pointing to the rocks.

"What?" Rebecca asked. "Another secret passage"

The King nodded, "Yes. It leads underground. Follow me!"

The King moved closer to the rocks, then stopped. He stared at them for a moment, then waved his hand back and forth in front of a crack between them. Suddenly, an opening appeared.

"Come," he said, moving towards the opening.

"I'm never getting used to this magic business!" Rebecca said, almost to herself.

Both Rebecca and Jimmy carried Ruth between them towards the opening between the rocks. It was dark inside as they entered. The King, in front of them, waved his hand again and light seemed to appear from nowhere along the walls of a passage.

"This way," the King said back to them as he began to walk along the passage. They followed him carrying Ruth between them as the passage twisted and turned. Finally, after some minutes, they came to a large cavern, just like the one they had been in before, only this one had caves surrounding the cavern in which the small people seemed to be living.

"What's this? Another refuge?" Rebecca asked, glancing around at the large underground cavern. Small people stepped out of the surrounding caves and came over to greet them. The moment they saw the King, people gasped in surprise and began to bow and kneel down in front of him.

"The King! The King! The King!"

The word spread around the cavern like wildfire and more and more people now came running out of the surrounding caves to kneel down in front of their King.

Rebecca saw Sev and her husband Roe come running out of one of the caves towards them.

"Reb!" Roe cried out with joy. "You and your friends are safe!"

Roe suddenly saw at the King, then knelt down in front of him next to Sev who was already kneeling.

"Your majesty!" Roe said. "We ... we thought you were dead!"

"Not quite yet," the King said, looking down at him. He looked at all of his people kneeling down before him, "These people," he said, gesturing back to Rebecca, Jimmy and Ruth, "are my friends! They helped me escape from the castle! See to them! Give them anything they desire! They are our honoured guests! Now ... rise!"

The people stood up and let out a cheer and cries of joy as they crowded around them.

Sev went to Rebecca, "Come! bring your friend Ru! We will tend to her!" she said.

Rebecca nodded and, with Jimmy's help, went through the cheering crowd carrying Ruth. They followed Sev over to one of the surrounding caves and went inside.

"Lay her down here," Sev said, pointing down at some blankets which lay on the floor. Both Rebecca and Jimmy laid Ruth down gently onto the blankets and covered her.

"What is wrong with her?" Sev asked kneeling down beside her.

Rebecca knelt down and stroked Ruth's head gently, "I think she has a fever! They ... tortured her! Used her for ... for entertainment!"

Sev looked up at Rebecca, then nodded, "I see," she said.

Sev turned and called out and two short women entered the small cave.

"My friends will see to her," Sev said.

She stood up, "Come, we must talk."

Rebecca stood up and followed her out of the cave with Jimmy beside her.

Sev sat down on a flat rock just outside the cave and gestured for them to do the same.

"What of the Darkness?" she asked. "What did you find?"

"We ... we found a box," Rebecca said.

"More like a chest," Jimmy corrected, sitting beside her. "It was big!"

"And ... what was inside this ... chest?" Sev asked.

"It was ... strange," Rebecca said. "It was moving inside, like a ... a storm. Just like the one outside. Your King told us it can be stopped by using a key. The key will lock the box ..." she glanced at Jimmy, "or rather, chest, and contain the storm inside. He said it will stop the Darkness' powers."

"Ah! The black box!"

Rebecca glanced at Jimmy, "See? It's a box."

"Yes ... I have heard of it!" Sev said. "But nobody has ever seen inside it. The King must have discovered this before they imprisoned him. We ... we heard that he was dead."

"The King said that the key is hung around the Darkness' neck," Rebecca said. "He said that it was impossible to get to."

Sev lowered her eyes, "Yes ... the Darkness has strong powers. It would be impossible to take the key from him, and yet ... we must find a way!"

Jimmy glanced towards the small cave inside which Ruth was lying.

"Ruth isn't looking good," he said.

He turned to look at Rebecca, "I'm sorry. She ... she's nice."

Rebecca looked back at him, then nodded

"Thank you," she said.

Sev noticed Jimmy's concern for Ruth and gazed at him with a smile on her lips.

Jimmy smiled back at her as if he were embarrassed, then glanced down, avoiding her eyes before speaking, "They found us once," he said. "Maybe because we were with you. We put your lives in danger."

Sev continued observing him, then reached across and touched his arm gently, "Our lives are always in danger," she said. "Ever since the Darkness arrived. To throw you out would be to cast out the goodness in our hearts and become like him, dark and unfeeling. It is love and caring that gives us light, it is for that we live, not to become beings of darkness, for we would prefer to die than live in darkness, with darkness in our hearts"

"There was a... a torture chamber," Jimmy said, glancing back up at her. "In the castle, did ... did the King torture people? As a punishment? Before the Darkness came?"

Sev smiled at him again, "That chamber hasn't been used for centuries," she said. "That belonged to our ancestors. Our people have evolved since then, as most people do."

Jimmy nodded, understandingly.

"Thank you," Sev said, looking at them both. "Thank you for saving our King."

"And thank you for trying to rid us of the Darkness!" Roe said, walking over to them with the King at his side. "Even if you did not succeed, you tried."

The King nodded as he looked at them, "And that is something we will never forget," he said.

*

The six horsemen rode through the forest followed by Krawl. Krawl grumbled wiping the rain from his face, "I hate riding!" he complained to himself, careful to keep his voice low in case one of the horsemen heard him. "Especially in the rain!"

Suddenly, one of the horsemen stopped in front of him.

Krawl rode forward, "What is it?" he asked.

"A strange feeling," the lead horseman said, looking at a clearing in front of them. "I feel the King's imprint. They are nearby."

The lead horseman rode forward circling the clearing, then stopped. "He uses magic!" the horseman said, turning back to Krawl.

Lightning flashed in the dark sky above and thunder rumbled loudly as the horseman raised his arm slowly and pointed to a crack between the rocks in front of him

"It is there!" he said.

Krawl looked towards the rock and saw nothing.

"A magical door?" he asked.

The lead horseman opened his hand, pointing it at the rock, and then a red beam of light shot out from his hand towards the crack. The beam seemed to hit an invisible shield of some sort. The shield was strong and seemed to be fighting against the red beam, forcing it back away from it. The lead horseman grunted as he tried with all his strength to keep the beam on the invisible shield, and then he broke through it with a gasp and the invisible shield disappeared.

Krawl rode forward, staring down at the crack between the rocks and the now visible opening into a secret passage.

"Time to pay a visit!" he said, with a grin.

CHAPTER 25

Tol was angry once again.

He walked back and forth throwing his arms up in the air and complaining.

"Oh! So they helped the King to escape! I still say it's dangerous to keep them here! Look what happened last time!"

"The King owes them his life, his freedom!" Roe said, sitting on a flat rock in a small alcove. "They are our guests!"

"Guests! Ha!" Tol stopped in front of him and pointed a finger down at Roe's face.

"They are a danger! You mark my words! It would be best to get rid of them! Now!"

Roe stood up and stared at him.

"Then go speak to the King! See if he agrees with you!"

Tol stared back at him, then lowered his head, "The King ..."

"The King will not listen to you!" Roe said, speaking before Tol could finish his sentence.

Tol sighed, then sat down on the flat rock gazing down at the ground.

"I ... I know," he said.

He glanced at Roe, "I just want to make sure that our people are safe," he said.

Roe smiled and placed his hand on Tol's shoulder.

"I know," he said. "I know you do, Tol. You're hot-headed sometimes, but you have good intentions."

Tol nodded, gazing back down at the ground.

"Thank you, my friend," he said.

Suddenly, Roe seemed to stiffen. He raised his hand, then stepped towards the entrance of the small alcove and looked across the cavern towards the far wall.

"Something has happened!" he said. "They are here!"

Tol looked at him, then stood up.

"Wha ...?" he started to say, moving over to the alcove's entrance, and then saw a movement on the other side of the cavern far to the right.

One of the black-clothed horsemen appeared running into the cavern. There were screams and cries of horror as the horseman, now on foot, raced towards the crowds of small people standing and sitting around the cavern. As he ran towards them red lightning bolts of magic shot out of his hands. The small people cried out and began fleeing in panic running in all directions as other horsemen on foot also appeared, throwing red lightning bolts towards them. The bolts struck some of the people throwing them up in the air and across the cavern with a terrible force.

"Stand and fight! Stand and fight!" Roe called out to the running and frightened crowd.

Roe stood his ground with Tol beside him. He glanced to the left and saw the King also standing his ground nearby the caves and facing the approaching black garbed horsemen. People screamed running out of the surrounding caves in all directions.

Roe turned to Toll, "Save our guests!" he shouted.

Tol looked at him, "But ..."

"Save them!" Roe shouted to him.

Tol quickly turned and ran across the cavern floor towards the cave where Rebecca and Jimmy had come to the entrance to see what was happening.

Sev appeared behind them both, pushing them forward, "You must go!" she was shouting. "You must go!"

Rebecca turned to her, "But ... Ruth!" Rebecca said, turning to run back to where her friend was lying on the ground, covered with blankets and unconscious with fever.

"No!" Sev said, grabbing Rebecca's hand. "You must save yourselves! Now go!"

Tol reached them.

"This way!" he said, pointing to the left.

Jimmy stood watching as both Roe and the King raised their hands towards the approaching horsemen. A magical yellow light came from their hands speeding towards the horsemen. The King's beam of light hit one horsemen and the horseman cried out staggering backwards. Red lightning bolts quickly shot out of the horsemen's hands blocking Roe's beam of yellow light, stopping the beam's energy from hitting them.

"Come!" Tol cried out, grabbing Jimmy's arm and pulling him to the left.

Reluctantly Jimmy followed, running behind Tol as Tol led him and Rebecca across the cavern to the left towards another passage. The screams from the cavern sounded behind them as they ran through the narrow entrance and along the dimly-lit passage, following its twists and turns until the sounds of the screaming faded and they came to a point of light at the far end. Tol led them forward and touched the wall to the right and the point of light grew larger as the rock wall in front of them seemed to shimmer then disappear.

They stepped out from the passage and into the light. It was daytime, and although there were still dark clouds rolling overhead and it was still raining, it seemed a little lighter than before. They followed behind Tol as he ran through the forest and then he led them out into a clearing and up a small rise. They stood on top looking down at the beach and the ocean on the other side.

"Where is the entrance to your world?" Tol asked.

Both Rebecca and Jimmy looked at him.

"Your world! The entrance! Where is it?" Tol demanded again impatiently..

Jimmy and Rebecca glanced at each other.

Rebecca shrugged, "We ... we don't even know how we got here!" she said.

"I ... I think it's somewhere near here," Jimmy said, glancing around.

"Bah!" Tol said, waving his arms angrily at them both. "Useless! You're both useless! Troublesome and useless!"

He glanced down at the landscape on the other side of the slope and looked across a large field. Far to the right he saw the huge triangular doorway which led into another world. In front of it were four armed creatures obviously standing guard.

He stared at it, "Hmm," he said to himself, placing his hand to his chin thoughtfully.

Suddenly, he turned away from it waving his hands as if dismissing the idea that had come to him.

"Not that one!" he said, as if speaking to himself. "That's the gate the Darkness came through!"

He glanced at both Rebecca and Jimmy, observing them as they both stared down at the huge ocean waves crashing up onto the beach. "Roe would never forgive me," he muttered under his breath as he shook his head.

The guards, standing in front of the huge triangular gateway seemed to be staring at them. Tol looked back towards them and suddenly realized that they were staring.

He took a step back.

"Oh! We ... we must go! Now!" he said urgently.

Both Rebecca and Jimmy turned to him.

"Quickly!' Tol shouted, pointing along the rise on which they were standing, "Run!"

Both Rebecca and Jimmy saw the guards across the field and heard them shouting and pointing towards them. They turned and quickly ran along the top of the rise following behind Tol who was now running as fast as he could. Two of the guards were now shouting and running towards them.

"Whe ... where are we going?" Jimmy called out to Tol as he ran.

"The other way!" Tol called back with the sound of panic in his voice.

As they ran along the rise with the beach and ocean on one side of them and the large field on the other, Tol saw what looked like black cone-shaped swirling smoke pointing downwards and hovering over the field further along.

"Is that it?" he shouted, pointing towards it as he ran.

Rebecca saw the black swirling smoke and shouted back to him, "Yes! That's it! But ... it seems to be in a different place!"

"Who cares?" Tol shouted back to them. "This way! Hurry!"

They followed him as he ran down the slope and into the field. Tol glanced back as he ran and saw that the two guards were gaining on them.

"Faster!" he shouted back to Rebecca and Jimmy. "Run faster!"

They ran as fast as they could towards the black swirling smoke, both Jimmy and Rebecca overtaking Tol as he ran on his short stubby legs.

Tol glanced back, panicking as he ran, "They're gaining!" he shouted.

The two guards, who were running after them, had almost caught up to them when they reached the black swirling cone-like smoke in front of them. Without thinking Rebecca dived forward beneath it followed by Jimmy and quickly disappeared. Tol, who was still running behind them, called out to them as one of the guards almost grabbed him.

"Wait for me!" he shouted, and then dived forward under the swirling black mass. Both guards suddenly stopped and watched as Tol disappeared from sight. They remained still, staring at the swirling blackness in front of them, then they slowly stepped back and turned to leave.

CHAPTER 26

Rebecca was the first to fall into the room.

Jimmy followed almost bumping into her, and then came Tol. The three of them lay still breathing heavily after going through the strange sensation of being whisked through a dark corridor and thrown into another world.

Rebecca slowly stood up and looked around.

"Are we back?" she asked.

The room in which they had landed was dark, but a shaft of light stretched across the floor towards them from an open door.

"Whe ... where are we?" Tol asked nervously as he stood up looking around.

"I ... I think we're back in our world," Jimmy said, standing up beside him.

A noise came from outside the open door.

Suddenly, a dark shape appeared in the doorway. They stared at it, remaining still.

The shape moved aside and once again light came through the open door.

"Wha ... what was that?" Tol asked.

"I don't know," Rebecca said.

Tol shot her a glance, "You don't know? This is your world!"

Rebecca looked at him, "I guess we're going to find out," she said, "as that's the only way out of here."

"Are there ... are there monsters in your world?" Tol asked in a nervous voice.

"Not until 'you' got here," Rebecca answered.

Tol glanced up at her, then looked back towards the open doorway, "Funny!" he said.

He turned to look at Jimmy, "Your friend's funny!" he said, gesturing towards Rebecca.

"Are there monsters here?" Jimmy said, looking at Tol as he repeated Tol's question. "Yes," Jimmy continued, answering Tol's question seriously. "There are. But they usually look normal."

"Well," Rebecca said, with a sigh, "shall we go through it, see what's on the other side?"

"You first!" Tol said, glancing up at her.

"I'll go first," Jimmy said.

He moved forward slowly and then stopped when he reached the door.

"And what if ... it's not our world?" Jimmy said, glancing back at Rebecca who was now just behind him. "Maybe ... it's another world," Jimmy said, hesitating.

"Maybe," Rebecca said. She took a deep breath, then walked forward passing Jimmy and went through the open doorway and into the light of the other room.

It was a large room, strangely decorated with grotesque looking furniture and dark nightmarish-style pictures hanging on the walls.

"Wow!" Jimmy breathed, glancing around as he stepped into the room behind her. "This place is creepy!"

Tol stepped into the room and stopped. He seemed to be listening, and then he lifted his hand, "Someone is here, waiting for us,' he said. "I feel it."

Both Rebecca and Jimmy glanced at each other. Rebecca looked towards a closed door on the far side of the room and started towards it, then a noise sounded to their left. Each of them spun round and they saw a man standing nearby the wall, half hidden by a large macabre-looking piece of furniture.

Dr. Schultz grinned, staring across at them.

His eyes were piercing, cold.

"Welcome back!" he said.

He looked down at Tol, "Ah! I see you've brought a friend with you!"

A door opened to his left and Miss Wong stepped into the room.

"Put them in isolation!" the doctor ordered. "I have a few questions to ask them!"

The muscled-bound male worker Tony appeared, stepping into the room behind Miss Wong.

"With pleasure doctor!" he said, as he moved towards them.

Jimmy seemed to snarl, then without hesitation he ran forward and head-butted Tony in the stomach. Tony cried out and staggered back but managed to catch his breath. He picked Jimmy up in his strong arms and head-butted him in the face. Jimmy cried out as he fell back to the floor. Tol let out a yell and ran forward. With his mouth open he bit Tony on the leg and kept growling like a dog keeping his teeth imbedded into Tony's flesh. Tony cried out and managed to kick Tol away from him. Tol rolled on the floor and then he was up again and running forward to attack once more. This time he jumped up and bit Tony's neck with his arms around him. Jimmy, who had risen to his feet, let out a yell and charged towards Tony who was still trying to get rid of Tol who was clinging tightly to him and now biting Tony's ear. Jimmy bunched his right hand into a fist and hit Tony with all his might square on the nose. Tony cried out again as blood began to spout out of his nose.

"Let's go!" Jimmy shouted, turning to Rebecca.

Rebecca was staring at Dr. Schultz, her eyes widening in fear as she saw something beginning to happen to him. His body started to change, as if he were going through some kind of transformation. Black spikes began to appear all over his body, breaking through his clothes and his skin which turned a deep red and then his face began to change into what could only be described as that of a demon.

Rebecca screamed.

Horns now protruded from Dr. Schultz's head as his feet grew, breaking the shoes on his feet. Dr. Schultz stared at her, his eyes now shining bright red as if there were a light behind them. Rebecca seemed to be frozen in place as she stared with horror-filled eyes at the terrifying creature which was once Dr. Schultz standing in front of them.

Jimmy stared at the creature as if he were in a trance, then suddenly came to his senses. "Go!" he shouted to Rebecca.

He ran forward and grabbed Rebecca's hand, pushing Miss Wong out of the way as she approached them menacingly with a syringe held ready to inject them. Rebecca screamed again as she stared back at the demon-like figure in horror, allowing Jimmy to pull her forward and out of the room through the open door. As Jimmy ran he remembered seeing the same nightmarish creature moving through the darkened streets when he was a child. It was exactly the same! he thought. Suddenly he remembered Tol and stopped to glance back.

"Tol!" he called out urgently.

Tol jumped down off Tony who was now clutching at his ear and screaming painfully. He was about to run out through the open doorway when he saw Miss Wong move across in front of him. Her eyes stared down at him hatefully as she leaned forward and picked up the syringe she had dropped on the floor. Tol stepped back as she advanced towards him raising the syringe in her hand ready to plunge it into him.

Both Jimmy and Rebecca heard an inhuman-like growl and then saw the hideous demon-like creature that was once Dr. Schultz appear in the open doorway and stare towards them.

"Go!" Jimmy shouted, turning to push Rebecca along the corridor in front of him. Together than ran not daring to look back as they heard the creature behind them, chasing them and growling wildly. They reached the end of the corridor and pushed their way through the swing doors finding that they were in another corridor. They ran on, hearing the terrible inhuman-like growling sounds behind them.

"It's gaining on us!" Rebecca cried out, not daring to look back but hearing the growling sounds coming closer as they ran. They reached two more swing doors and ran through them. Jimmy suddenly stopped as he saw a mop leaning against the wall next to a bucket. He quickly ran over to the mop, picked it up and took it back to the swing doors. With only seconds to spare he pushed the long handle of the mop through the handles on the two swing doors. The creature hit the swing door windows in front of him with a force, growling wildly and making Jimmy jerk back away from the doors. With the long mop placed through the handles of the doors, the swing doors held fast. Both Jimmy and Rebecca now stood frozen, staring at the nightmarish creature which continued to growl at them savagely through the windows of the swing doors.

Jimmy turned to look at Rebecca who was still staring in shock at the horrible creature. He took her hand, "Let's go!" he said.

He pulled on Rebecca's hand, forcing her away from the swing doors and along the corridor.

"We have to find a way out!" Jimmy said, pulling Rebecca forward behind him. "That door may not hold it, whatever it is!"

They rounded a bend in the corridor, and then suddenly stopped in their tracks.

There, in front of them, stood a small boy. His face was pale, like a ghost. The boy remained still, staring at them.

Both Jimmy and Rebecca stared back at him. Jimmy felt Rebecca's hand in his beginning to shake in fear.

"It ... it's the ghost!" Rebecca said in a trembling voice.

"Ghost?" Jimmy repeated, gazing at the small boy strangely.

He let go of Rebecca's hand and moved slowly towards the boy.

Rebecca watched him, "Jimmy ...!" she called out.

Suddenly, the little boy raised his arm and, continuing to stare at them, pointed towards a short corridor on his left.

Jimmy glanced towards the corridor, then looked back at the boy.

"Who ... who are you?" he asked.

Just then, right before their eyes, the little boy disappeared.

Jimmy heard Rebecca gasped from behind him. They both remained still, staring at the spot where the boy had been standing.

"This ... this is nuts!" Jimmy said.

"Let's go!" Rebecca said, moving forward and grasping Jimmy's hand. "He ... he was pointing this way!"

Jimmy, still staring at the spot where the boy had disappeared, followed her into the short corridor the boy had pointed towards.

They stopped half-way along it seeing that it was a dead end.

"There ... there's no way out!" Jimmy said, glancing around at the walls. "Why ... why would he point this way?"

Rebecca looked around and saw a small flap-like door built into the wall on the right.

She went over to it.

"Jimmy!" she called. "Over here!"

Jimmy turned and ran over to her.

Rebecca opened the flap-like door and looked inside.

"What is it?" Jimmy asked.

"I think it's a chute," Rebecca said. "It's used for throwing away rubbish."

"What? Are we ... are we supposed to go down that? We don't know what's at the bottom!"

Suddenly, they heard the terrifying sound of the demon-like creature. It had obviously broken through the swing doors and was now running along the corridor they had left towards them.

"There's one way to find out!" Rebecca said.

"You go first!" Jimmy said to her.

Rebecca looked at him.

"Come on!" Jimmy said, lifting her up to help her get into the chute. Rebecca got into the chute, and then, before she could realize it, she was screaming and speeding down towards the bottom. Jimmy opened the chute's flap and climbed inside just as the demon-like monster came into sight growling wildly and running towards him. Jimmy let go of the grip he had and then fell, crying out as sped down the chute towards the bottom. It only took a few seconds before he dropped out of the chute and into the large container placed beneath it. He fell into a pile of dust and rubbish and was immediately thankful that the container was almost full with empty boxes. Jimmy sat up, coughing and wiping the dust from his face and clothes. He saw Rebecca who had already jumped out of the container and was brushing herself down. Jimmy grabbed the side of the container and pulled himself up and out of it, landing on the ground beside Rebecca.

"Whe ... where are we?" Jimmy managed to asked, wiping the dust from his mouth and nose.

"We're outside!" Rebecca said, now moving away from him and looking up at the dark clouds of the storm above them.

Jimmy raised his head, allowing the rain which was falling heavily to wash over his face.

Lightning streaked across the sky and thunder boomed loudly as Rebecca remained staring up at the dark storm-filled clouds.

"It looks like we may have a problem," she said.

CHAPTER 27

"Where are we going?" Jimmy asked, following Rebecca.

"To the police," Rebecca said, stopping at the crossroads at the end of the street.

"We'll go to the central police station," she said. "We'll tell them everything."

"Do you ... do you think that's a good idea? I mean ... what can the police do?"

Rebecca turned to look at him, "Do you have a better idea?" she asked.

Jimmy looked back at her, then shook his head.

"Do ... do you think they'll believe us?" Jimmy asked.

Rebecca gazed down thoughtfully, "Maybe not," she said. "But ... we have to tell someone! Anyway, we'll tell them about Dr. Schultz. Tell them he ... he's experimenting with people. They'd have to investigate!"

Rebecca looked both right and left. There were no cars on the road, no people in the street.

"That's strange," she said, gazing around.

They both stood for a moment looking at the deserted street.

"Come on!" Rebecca said, pointing across to the other side the street. "The metro station's over there."

They ran across the street, reached the entrance to the metro station and ran down the steps.

"Where is everybody?" Jimmy asked.

"I've no idea," Rebecca said, looking around as they reached the bottom of the staircase and ran across to the barriers. "But ... this is really weird!"

They jumped a barrier and ran down the steps to the platform.

The platform was completely deserted.

"Maybe there are no trains," Jimmy said, as they stood waiting on the deserted platform. Suddenly, they heard the sound of a train coming towards them through the dark tunnel. Its lights came into view and the air started to blow along the platform. The noise of the approaching train grew louder, and then it exited the tunnel like a long metal snake rolling noisily along the rails. The train went the length of the platform, and then it stopped. The doors slid open and both Rebecca and Jimmy got on. As the doors closed behind them, they looked at the other passengers. Every seat was taken and both Rebecca and Jimmy were the only passengers standing. As they looked at the other passengers, they noticed something strange. Every single passenger had his or her head bowed and were either studying something on their mobile phones or were studying a screen on their laptop computers or mini-coms.

Jimmy glanced at Rebecca, "What are they all looking at?" he asked.

"Everyone's into computers these days," Rebecca answered. "Computer games, chat, info ... it's very popular. Ellie, for example, is an addict."

Jimmy stared at all of the passengers in surprise.

"It's so ... quiet," he said.

Rebecca grinned, "Welcome to the modern world," she said.

Suddenly, as if all of the passengers had received the same signal at the same time, each one of them looked up from their computer screens and stared towards both Rebecca and Jimmy.

"Why ... why are they looking at us?" Jimmy asked.

Rebecca looked at each of the passengers as they stared at her and Jimmy with blank expressionless faces.

"I ... I don't know," she said. "Something's ... not right."

Then, as if directed by the same order, all of the passengers stood up, continuing to stare at them. Rebecca backed away, pulling on Jimmy's arm.

"I ... I think we should go," she said.

The passengers now began to walk towards them, still staring at them blankly, expressionlessly.

"Go! Go! Go!" Rebecca shouted, turning to run and pulling on Jimmy's arm.

Rebecca ran into the next carriage, pulling Jimmy behind her. The passengers in the second carriage were still sitting and staring at their mobile phones and computer screens, but as soon as Rebecca and Jimmy appeared, they all looked up and began staring at them. The train was now entering another station and Rebecca ran towards the nearest door still holding onto Jimmy's arm and pulling him behind her. The passengers from the previous carriage appeared, coming through the adjoining carriage door, as the passengers in the second carriage were now beginning to stand up and move towards Rebecca and Jimmy. As the train rolled along the platform of the next station Rebecca beat at the doors nervously.

"Come on! Come on! Come on!" she shouted. "Open up! Open up!"

Jimmy glanced back at the passengers who were moving slowly towards them and getting closer. Something strange seemed to be shining in their eyes. A snarl now appeared on their faces as they began to growl menacingly, raising their arms and reaching out to grab them.

"Come on!" Rebecca shouted, banging on the doors.

The train finally came to a stop and the doors slid open. Both Rebecca and Jimmy leapt out onto the platform and began to run for the stairs leading up towards the station's exit. Jimmy glanced back as they reached the top of the stairs and saw the passengers now beginning to mount the stairs slowly behind them.

"Go!" he shouted, turning to Rebecca "They're right behind us!"

Together, they ran along a corridor, reached the barriers and jumped over them, then they ran up the stairs of the exit to the outside. When they reached the street level at the top of the stairs they stopped in their tracks looking around. They saw that they were completely surrounded by a crowd of people standing still in the street and staring at them with blank, expressionless faces. Both Rebecca and Jimmy stood looking at them. The people's eyes seemed strange, unfocused, and then suddenly, as if on command, they all began to growl like they were wild vicious beasts.

CHAPTER 28

"What do we do?" Jimmy asked.

Rebecca stared at the surrounding people. Each of them was snarling and growling viciously towards them. On the staircase behind Rebecca and Jimmy, more people, also growling, were coming up towards them. Suddenly, Rebecca noticed an abandoned skateboard on the pavement. The surrounding people began moving forward as Rebecca bent and picked up the skateboard.

"Stay behind me!" she said to Jimmy.

"Wha ... what are you going to do?" Jimmy asked.

Suddenly, without answering, Rebecca ran forward holding the skateboard high in her hands and hit the first person she came to. It was a woman in her forties. The woman fell without crying out as if she hadn't felt anything. Rebecca swung the board again and hit the man she'd been standing next to. The man fell from a blow to the head and landed on the ground beside the woman who was now attempting to get up.

"Come on!" Rebecca cried out, jumping over the two people she'd knocked down and throwing the skateboard to the side.

She managed to get through the gap between the other people but as Jimmy tried to jump through the gap behind her hands reached out to grab him. Jimmy let out a cry as hands on both sides of him grabbed at his clothes. Rebecca turned back and kicked the man grabbing Jimmy on his left. The man fell as Jimmy tried to pull away from the man grabbing at his clothes from the right.

"Leave him alone!" Rebecca cried out.

She pulled Jimmy towards her and then Jimmy broke free from the other man's grip.

"Come on!" Rebecca shouted, pulling on Jimmy's hand as they fled from the zombie-like group of people towards the other end of the street. They ran as fast as they could, then turned a corner and stopped to catch their breath.

"Are ... are they still after us?" Rebecca asked, breathing heavily.

Jimmy turned and glanced around the corner.

"They're coming this way," he said. "But they're moving slowly."

"Good ... " Rebecca said. "We ... we can outrun them!"

Jimmy looked at her.

"Thanks," he said.

Rebecca smiled at him and nodded, "It's okay!" she said, still breathing heavily.

"Wha ... what do you think happened to them?" Jimmy asked. "What's happened to the world?"

Rebecca leaned back against the wall, "The ... the Darkness," she said. "He must be here, controlling."

"But ... we left him back in the other world!"

Rebecca shook her head, "We can't think about that right now. Let's just get to the central police station."

"What for?" Jimmy asked. "If this world's been taken over, they'll be like everybody else."

"We have to try!" Rebecca said. "We ... we don't have much choice. Come on, it's just a few blocks away now."

Rebecca turned to walk quickly along the street.

Jimmy stared after her.

"Come on!" Rebecca said, turning to look back at him.

Jimmy shrugged with a sigh, "Okay, but I don't think it will do much good."

He began to follow her along the quiet deserted street, occasionally glancing back to see if the crowd of people they had broken through had yet reached the corner. Strangely enough, they did not appear. It was as if they had given up the chase. After some minutes, Rebecca and Jimmy came to a flyover. They were just walking towards it when they saw a crowd of people turning a corner further down along the street that they were on.

"Come on! This way!" Rebecca said, running over to stand against the wall under the flyover. Jimmy followed her and they both stood with their backs to the wall hidden from sight as the crowd of people passed by, walking slowly along the street with their eyes glazed as if they were hypnotized. Both Rebecca and Jimmy waited until they had passed, then they emerged from beneath the flyover and began to run in the opposite direction. They had almost reached the central police station when they saw another crowd of people. One group of people was standing outside the police station as if they were waiting, while another group of people were walking along the street directly towards them. Rebecca pulled on Jimmy's arm and crouched down to hide behind a parked car.

"They're everywhere!" Jimmy said.

Rebecca leaned back against the car.

If you've got any ideas," she said, "now's the time to tell me."

Jimmy glanced around the street. As he was doing so, he heard someone call over to them. He looked towards the sound on the opposite side of the street and saw the public library. A man was standing at one of the open windows calling out to them. Jimmy tapped on Rebecca's arm and pointed towards the library. Rebecca looked and saw the man standing at the open window.

"Over here!" the man called out, waving for them to come over.

Jimmy glanced at Rebecca, "What do you think?" he asked.

Rebecca stared across the street at the man standing behind the open window of the library.

"I don't think we have much choice!" she said.

Jimmy glanced around the car at the approaching group of people walking slowly in their direction.

"How far away are they?" Rebecca asked.

"If we go now," Jimmy said, "we should make it over to the library."

"But they'll see us?"

Jimmy nodded, "Wherever we go, they're going to see us," he said.

Rebecca nodded, "Okay," she said.

She took a deep breath, then got up, "Go!" she shouted, turning to run towards the library. Jimmy stood up and followed her. They ran across the street as fast as they could. Jimmy glanced back as they ran and saw the heads of the people who had been walking towards them turn in their direction. Just before they reached the library door, the door open allowing them to pass through inside.

The man who had opened the door for them quickly closed it behind them, then he turned to them and smiled.

"Welcome to the library!" he said.

CHAPTER 29

Mr. Svelt was a stout man in his fifties. He had grey hair and a grey beard and introduced himself as the chief librarian. He showed both Rebecca and Jimmy through to the library where a group of about ten people were sitting around at various tables. The people looked up as they came in.

"We have more members for our group," Mr. Svelt said to them, gesturing towards Rebecca and Jimmy who were following behind him.

"What's going on out there?" one young man asked, looking towards Rebecca. "Are there others? Like us?"

Rebecca stared at him, not really sure what to answer.

Mr. Svelt looked at her, "We've been here since the change," he said. "We don't know what's happening outside, just how far this ... this change has spread."

Rebecca looked at him, "Change?" she repeated.

"Zombies!" a young girl sitting at a table said. "Mr. Svelt means zombies! There are zombies out there and we're stuck in here!"

Mr. Svelt turned to her, "They're not ... what you would technically call, zombies," he said. "At least, not like those dreadful flesh eating ones you see in those horror films." "Maybe not," the girl said, "but they're still zombies!"

Mr. Svelt looked back at Rebecca and Jimmy, "In fact ... we don't really know what they are."

"I call them possessed," the young man who had spoken earlier said. "It's like something's in their minds, in their souls, possessing them!"

Mr. Svelt nodded, "That may be closer to the truth, yes."

"Well?" the young man said, looking once again at Rebecca, "You didn't answer my question. Are they everywhere? We can't be the only ones left in the city who are normal, right?"

Rebecca shrugged, "I ... I don't know," she said. "We ... we've just arrived."

Everyone stared at them, including Mr. Svelt.

"From where?" Mr. Svelt asked.

Rebecca glanced at Jimmy who was standing quietly beside her, then looked back at Mr. Svelt.

"That ... that's a long story," she said.

"What do you mean, a long story?" the young man asked, sounding annoyed as he spoke. "All you have to do is tell us where you came from!"

Rebecca stared back at him in silence, not sure if she should tell them where they had been, not sure if they would even believe her. In the silence that followed, Mr. Svelt stepped forward and took Rebecca's hand. He turned to look at the young man.

"I think that will be enough questions for now," he said. "I fear that our guests may have been traumatized enough as it is."

He glanced back at Rebecca and Jimmy and gave them a pleasing smile, "Come, we have food and drinks," he said, gesturing for them to follow him across the library floor to the far side.

He called back as they went, "Becky! Will you come and see to our guests?"

Becky, the dark haired girl who had spoken earlier, stood up from the table where she had been sitting with the group of people.

"Sure," she said, coming over to join them as Mr. Svelt led both Rebecca and Jimmy to a table with various food and drinks on it.

"Please, sit down," Mr. Svelt said, gesturing towards the chairs around the table.

Both Rebecca and Jimmy sat down looking at the food and drinks in front of them. Becky reached the table and sat down in front of them.

"Want a drink?" she asked, picking up a bottle of soda drink and placing two paper cups down in front of them.

They both nodded.

"Thank you," Rebecca said, picking up the cup after Becky had poured them both drinks.

Becky leaned forward, staring at them both as Rebecca picked up a sandwich and Jimmy opened a packet of crisps and started placing the crisps into what looked like a hamburger.

"How long have you been here?" Rebecca asked, gazing across at Becky.

Becky continued to stare at Jimmy who was now eating his crisp filled hamburger as if he hadn't eaten for a week.

"It's been four days now," Becky said.

Both Rebecca and Jimmy glanced at each other.

"F ... four days?" Jimmy repeated.

"We ... couldn't have been gone that long," Rebecca said, looking at him. "could we?"

Jimmy stared down, shaking his head, "I ... I don't know," he said. "It ... it didn't feel like four days."

Becky leaned further forward, listening to them both.

"What's going on?" she asked softly. "Where did you two go?"

Neither Rebecca nor Jimmy said anything for a moment. They both sat gazing down thoughtfully, as if they were trying to understand something. Finally, Rebecca looked up and stared across a Becky.

"We ... we went to another world," she said.

Becky stared back at her, then leaned back in her chair, "Oh, come on! You're kidding!" she said. "You ... you 'are' kidding, right?"

"No,' Jimmy said, looking at her. "It's true!"

"Somehow we ... were transported into another world," Rebecca said.

Becky stared at them both open-mouthed.

"I'm not sure how long we were there," Rebecca continued, "but ... it certainly didn't feel like four days."

Becky remained staring at them both in silence for a moment.

"Okay, let's ... let's say I believe you. How ... er, how did you get there?" she asked. "What was the other world like? Is that where ... these things come from?"

"What things?" Jimmy asked.

Becky looked at him, "We've all seen them, every one of us here in the library," she said. "I saw one when I was younger, nobody else saw it, but I did. Of course, nobody believed me! I ... I couldn't understand why I saw it, when nobody else did."

Jimmy stared at her.

"What things?" Rebecca asked. "What were they?"

"Monsters," Becky said. "Grotesque looking monsters, moving in the shadows, appearing in the night."

Jimmy continued staring at her, his mouth opening as if he were in shock.

"Long fingers?" he asked. "With nails like claws? Red eyes that seemed to glow?"

Becky looked at him, "You've seen them too?" she asked.

"When I was a child," Jimmy said.

"And ... " he was about to continue.

"And just a few hours ago," Rebecca said, finishing his sentence for him, "we were chased by one. It was a ... a person before. A doctor, and then ... he changed, transformed into this ... this monster!"

"You see?" Becky said. "Everyone in this library has seen them, even Mr. Svelt, the chief librarian has seen them. What ... what I don't understand is ... why other people didn't see them."

Rebecca remembered the ghost of the little boy that both she and Jimmy had seen, and yet previously, when she had seen it for the first time, her friend Ruth couldn't see anything.

Rebecca glanced at Mr. Svelt and the other people sitting at a large table on the other side of the library.

"Everyone has seen them?" she said, as if to herself. "No one here has changed like the people outside ... why?"

She stood up and walked across to the other table. Mr. Svelt and the others looked up at her as she came over, followed by both Jimmy and Becky.

"Why didn't it affect us?" she asked, looking down at Mr. Svelt. "What do we all have in common that those outside don't?"

Thomas, the young man who had spoken earlier gazed at her strangely, "Well ... 'some' of us were affected," he said.

"Thomas is right, Mr. Svelt said. "We put five people in a room and locked the door. We've been discussing why, in this library, those five were affected and not us."

"At first, we thought that the library was protected," a young girl said. "Then ... five of us in here changed, just like the people outside."

"There must be a reason," Rebecca said. "A reason why most people changed and others didn't."

Mr. Svelt nodded, "Granted, we all agree with you. But ... what is the reason?"

"That's the million dollar question," Thomas said. "Why?"

CHAPTER 30

Rebecca stared through the small round window of the door at the five 'changed' library members in the locked room.

Becky came along the corridor to join her.

"How are you doing?" she asked.

Rebecca glanced at her, "I'm fine," she said.

Mr. Svelt says we have enough food to last us at least two days, then things will get difficult. He says that someone will have to go out and try to bring back some food and drinks. My friend Thomas and your friend Jimmy have volunteered."

Rebecca looked at her with a worried expression, she was suddenly afraid for Jimmy.

"They just sit there," Becky said, gazing through the door's glass window and into the room where the five people were being kept. "It's like ... they're waiting for something."

"There must be a reason," Rebecca said thoughtfully. "Why they changed and nobody else in the library did."

She turned to Becky, "Did they eat or drink anything special?"

Becky shrugged, "No, we all ate and drank the same stuff."

Rebecca sighed, placing her head against the door.

"There must be a reason," she said again.

After a moment's silence, she looked at Becky.

"How ... how did it happen?" she asked. "I mean ... how did it begin? The people ... what you call the zombie affect?"

Becky leaned against the door.

"Well, first there was the staring, which ... just never seems to go away apparently. Then, the children began to disappear."

"The children?" Rebecca repeated.

'Yes, they ... they took the children first. Then ... they started rounding up the homeless."

Rebecca stared at her.

"The children ... and the homeless?" she said, as if thinking carefully.

Suddenly, her eyes widened, "The children and the homeless!" she said again.

She turned and ran past Becky and back into the library's large reading room to where the others were still sitting at a table and discussing.

"The children!" she said, looking down at Mr. Svelt. "And the homeless!"

Mr. Svelt stared up at her.

"What about the children and the homeless?" he asked.

"They took them first!" Rebecca said.

"So?" Thomas asked, looking up at her.

"Jimmy saw one when he was a child, and Becky did too! When you are a child, you notice things, see things that adults don't see."

Everyone stared at her in silence for a moment.

"Er ... Mr. Svelt is not a child," Thomas pointed out. "And I never saw one when I was a child."

"But you have seen them!" Rebecca said. "Everyone in this room has seen them!"

She pointed back in the direction of the room where the five people were being kept.

"What did they do that you didn't do before they changed?" she asked.

"Look ... Thomas said. "We all did the same things ... we read books! We're in a library for God's sake!"

Mr. Svelt stared thoughtfully, then turned to him, "Wait a minute ... that's not entirely true."

"What do you mean?" Thomas asked.

"We have computers here," Mr. Svelt said. "They were reading books online."

Everyone looked at each other.

"Robert wasn't," Becky said. "He ... didn't like reading books."

"That's right," said another girl. "Every time he came here he seemed to fall asleep. His teacher forced him to come here for his studies. What he really liked doing was playing computer games and watching TV."

Mr. Svelt stood up, "Computers!" he said. "Television!"

Thomas looked at him, "Do ... do you mean that because we're reading ... we're not affected by this?"

Mr. Svelt turned to him

"No ... what I mean, is that because you don't use computers or watch TV, you're not affected by this!"

Rebecca looked a Jimmy who was standing quietly, listening.

"Jimmy," she said. "Do you read books?"

Jimmy hesitated for a moment looking down sheepishly, then he glanced up at her.

"No," he said.

"Do you use computers or watch TV?" Thomas asked.

Jimmy shook his head, "No," he said.

Becky studied him.

"My God! ... What did you do for fun?" she asked in amazement.

Jimmy looked at her.

"No fun, just ...try to survive," he said. "Everyday."

Rebecca looked at the other people.

"Jimmy ... lived on the streets," she said.

CHAPTER 31

Mr. Svelt sat at a table going through a very thick and very old book looking for something.

"So, what do we do now?" Thomas asked, standing near the bookshelves and looking down at him.

"One moment Thomas," Mr. Svelt said, turning a few more pages to study something he'd found in the book.

He glanced up, "You say they call it the 'Darkness'?" he asked Rebecca.

Rebecca, who was standing on the other side of the table, nodded, "Yes," she said.

"This ... door, or gateway you say you saw. People were being herded into it, and then ... they disappeared?"

"That's right," Rebecca said.

Mr. Svelt sighed, then began going through the book once more.

"I've seen something like this ... " Mr. Svelt said. "In one of these books. I'm sure I have!"

"There were guards," Jimmy said. "They ... didn't look human. They had ... spears! Or ... something that looked like spears."

"Is this going to help us?" Thomas asked, impatiently. "I mean ... we've got to 'do' something, right?"

Mr. Svelt glanced up at him.

"If we can find out what this is ... if this has been seen before ... then we have a better chance of knowing what to do about it."

Thomas sighed, then shrugged, "Okay! Okay!" He turned and leaned against the nearby bookcase.

"Here! I've found it!" Mr. Svelt said suddenly as he saw the page in the book that he was looking for.

Thomas, Rebecca and Jimmy immediately went over to him to gaze down at the book.

Mr. Svelt's finger was showing a picture of what looked like a huge triangular doorway which seemed to lead into another world. A strange looking guard was standing beside it holding a spear-like weapon and at least six people were in the picture being led towards the doorway by two other guards. To the right, in the distance, they saw a dark figure dressed completely in black, his face hidden beneath a hood.

"It says here that the Darkness comes and takes souls into his world," Mr. Svelt said. "He can do this through sleep, in dreams which are not dreams, but real, or in other ways. He takes believers, those who dabble in magic, black magic, and those who are ... weak, easily influenced."

"In the world we went to," Rebecca said, "there was no TV, there were no computers, but they 'did' do magic."

"There are those who do black magic even in this world," Mr. Svelt said. "But with its computers and TV ... this world must have been an easy target. The people would be ... easy to influence on a mass scale the world over!"

"You mean ... kind of like hypnosis?" Thomas asked.

Mr. Svelt glanced up at him and nodded, "Easily," he said.

"Great!" Thomas said. "Does it tell us how to fight this ... Darkness? How are we supposed to stop it?"

Mr. Svelt looked back down at the book and read what was written on the page beside the picture.

"It says ... the Darkness can be defeated by light."

They each stared down at the book.

"Is that all?" Thomas said, after a moment. "Nothing else? It just says ... light? Hell, this is going to be easy! All we have to do is each of us shine a torch towards it! Light? Are you kidding me? I mean ... what the hell! Do you really think that shining a light on it is going to work?"

Thomas walked away in disgust.

"This is useless!" he said, as he went.

The others watched him walk away, then glanced down once again at the book.

"Who wrote this?" Rebecca asked. "Where does the picture come from? Mr. Svelt turned the book over to show her the cover. It was an old book, its cover was almost falling apart.

"It originates from ancient scriptures," he said. "Probably copied into this book. Difficult to say how old the book is exactly, or the original scriptures, but they 'are' very, very old."

"This light," Rebecca said, turning the book over to glance down once again at the picture. "What do you think it means?"

Mr. Svelt stared down at the picture thoughtfully, "I don't know," he said, shaking his head. "But ... the light it talks about ... it can't just be an ordinary light."

"They're coming!" Becky suddenly shouted, turning from the window where she had been standing and gazing out into the street.

"A whole crowd of them!" she shouted. "They're coming!"

Mr. Svelt stood up.

Suddenly something came crashing through the library window. All of the people moved back away from the windows, and then the other windows were also broken.

Shouting came from outside and then people started climbing through the broken windows and into the library. The people in the library screamed and turned to run, but the people who had climbed in through the windows, although still having a glazed look in their eyes, were now moving faster than they had before.

"Quickly!" Mr. Svelt cried out. "The back! Go through the back!"

Both Rebecca and Jimmy followed him, running across the library floor towards the corridor leading to a back exit. They heard screams behind them as they ran through the corridor, and then they reached the door at the end. Mr. Svelt fumbled with his keys as both Thomas and Becky came running along the corridor to join them. Mr. Svelt found the right key, unlocked the door, and then ran outside followed by the others. Two men appeared in front of them. Mr., Svelt pushed one of them aside as Thomas hit the other. They ran past them as rain poured down from a dark sky and lightning flashed overhead, accompanied by the booming sound of loud thunder.

CHAPTER 32

"This way!" Thomas cried out, running along the street through the heavy pouring rain towards a large white building on the left.

The others followed him.

Jimmy saw that they were running towards a hospital. An ambulance stood outside its main entrance with all of its doors open. It was completely empty. They ran into the hospital and saw a mess of papers and chairs which lay upturned on the floor.

"Why the hospital?" Rebecca asked, breathing heavily as she stopped to catch her breath.

"It gets us out of the rain!" Thomas said, glancing across at her. "And besides, I don't really know where else to go!"

Mr. Svelt went around behind the reception desk and tried the phone.

"Dead," he said. "Just like the one in the library."

Becky tried turning on her mobile phone. It came on with a high-pitched whistling noise.

"Turn it off!" Mr. Svelt called out, staring at her. "We've no idea of what those signals are doing to the brain! We could ... "

"Become like them?" Rebecca said, finishing his sentence for him.

Mr. Svelt looked at her.

"Yes ... yes, exactly!"

Becky quickly turned off her mobile phone and gazed around the hospital reception hall.

"I get the feeling we're the only normal people in the world!" she said.

Rebecca shook her head, "No, there must be others. If not in this city, then in other cities, in other countries."

"Maybe not for long, "Thomas said. "Whatever controls the people will certainly be out to get us!"

Thomas is right," Mr. Svelt said. "We must think of a plan ... something. We've got to stop this!"

"How can we do anything?" Becky asked. "There are only five of us!"

"There must be a way!" Mr. Svelt said.

"Yeah, well maybe we should just be thinking about how to survive!" Thomas said. "Because, Mr. Svelt, I can't see anything that we can do against them!"

"You said that a light can destroy the Darkness," Rebecca said, looking at Mr. Svelt.

Mr. Svelt nodded, "That's what the book said."

"The book?" Thomas said. "The book? You don't believe what was written in that book, do you? I mean, a light? What the hell is that even supposed to mean?"

Rebecca turned to him, "It's all we have," she said. "We'll have to try to figure it out!"

Thomas shook his head, "Well, good luck with that!" he said. "I'm going to look around, see if I can find something more useful than just a light!"

Thomas walked away across the littered reception floor towards a corridor.

"He's frustrated," Mr. Svelt said, watching him leave.

"We all are," Rebecca said.

She turned to look at Jimmy who was still standing by the main entrance looking out at the rain.

"You see anything?" she asked, walking over to him.

Jimmy shook his head, "No."

"Maybe they won't come," she said.

"They'll come," Jimmy said. "They're bound to."

Rebecca looked at him.

"You're pretty calm about this. I mean, there's Thomas freaking out, but you ... "

Jimmy looked back at her.

He shrugged, "Guess I've always been moving, always running, one way or another," he said.

Rebecca stared at him, then nodded, "Right," she said. "By the way, your stuttering has improved. Shock therapy?"

Jimmy smiled at her, "Maybe," he said.

Rebecca smiled back at him.

"Hey!" Becky called out from nearby the reception desk. "My mobile! It ... it just came on by itself!"

The others looked at her and saw that she was holding her mobile phone in her hand.

A light seemed to be coming from it. Becky stared down at the images being sent. Her eyes widened.

"My God! ... It's ... "

There was a high-pitched sound which grew louder, and then the phone exploded in her hand.

Becky screamed falling back from the explosion, her hand now a bloody mess as she fell to the floor writhing and screaming in pain. Rebecca and Jimmy ran over to her as Mr. Svelt ran around towards her from behind the reception desk. They saw three of her fingers lying in a bloody mess on the floor beside her as she continued screaming and writhing on the floor uncontrollably.

"Aaaaaaaaargh!!!"

The three of them knelt down beside her.

"Oh my God!" Mr. Svelt exclaimed, staring down at the bloody mess on the floor from the injury to Becky's hand.

He tried to stop her from moving, tried to calm her, but she continued screaming and writhing around on the floor in pain. Lightning flashed and thunder crashed outside the hospital, but there was something else, something much more frightening. Jimmy glanced round. He was sure that he saw something moving. He jumped up and ran back over to the hospital's main entrance and gazed out into the rain.

"They're coming!" he cried back to Rebecca and Mr. Svelt. "They're coming!"

He ran back over to them.

"Help me get her up!" Mr. Svelt shouted, lifting the screaming and writhing Becky up off the floor. Both Rebecca and Jimmy helped him lift her up.

"Come on! This way!" Mr. Svelt shouted, guiding Becky, who was grasping at her bloody hand in agony and continuing to scream.

They ran over to the corridor that Thomas had taken, leaving a trail of blood on the floor behind them as they went.

A mob of people burst through the hospital's main entrance, some of them shouting and others growling as if they were wild animals. They saw the fresh blood stains leading across the floor and sniffed as if they were smelling the blood, then they ran forward, shouting and growling louder towards the corridor.

CHAPTER 33

"I can't! I can't" Becky cried as she stumbled.

Mr. Svelt tried to pull her up.

"Leave me!" Becky said, grasping her bloody hand painfully in front of her. "I can't go on! Leave me!"

"No!" Mr. Svelt shouted, kneeling beside her.

Both Rebecca and Jimmy ran back to help him pick her up. Suddenly they saw the shouting and growling mob running along the corridor towards them.

"Leave me!" Becky cried again.

"I won't leave you!" Mr. Svelt shouted, staring towards the approaching mob.

He turned to both Rebecca and Jimmy.

"You go! Go! Get out of here!" he shouted.

"But ..." Rebecca began.

"I said go!" Mr. Svelt shouted again pushing Rebecca away.

Jimmy pulled on Rebecca's arm, "Let's go!" he said, staring at the mob running along the corridor towards them.

Together they turned and began running along the corridor away from the approaching mob leaving Becky and Mr. Svelts behind them. Becky continued crying and grasping at her injured hand as Mr. Svelt stroked her face gently. He raised his head, then stood up to face the shouting and growling people running towards them. As both Rebecca and Jimmy ran along the hospital corridor in the other direction, they heard the screams from behind them. Rebecca glanced back and saw both Mr. Svelt and Becky disappear behind the mob of people who had reached them and were now beating them savagely.

"Come on!" Jimmy called back to her, pulling on her arm again.

They ran the length of the corridor, leaving the mob behind them, then turned a corner to the left and stopped.

Jimmy peeked back around the corner

"Are they still coming?" Rebecca asked..

A hand suddenly touched Rebecca's shoulder and she spun round with a scream.

Thomas stood there looking at them both.

"Hey! It's only me!" he said. "Whe ... where are Mr. Svelt and Becky?"

"They ... they got caught," Rebecca said.

Thomas stared at her, then glanced down sadly.

"Oh my God!" he said softly to himself.

Jimmy peeked back around the wall into the other corridor they'd just left.

"They're coming!" he said.

.

"This way!" Thomas said, turning and pointing towards a door on the right.

They followed him across the corridor and into a room. It was dimly lit, and like the reception hall, the floor was littered with papers and other rubbish. Thomas led them over to a window and opened it.

"We can't stay here any longer!" he said.

Rebecca nodded in agreement.

Thomas climbed out through the window first and into the pouring rain outside followed by both Rebecca and Jimmy.

"Where do we go now?" Thomas asked, glancing back at them once they were all outside.

Rebecca looked at him for a moment, then moved forward to pass him.

"Follow me!" she said.

*

They stopped beside the park staring across at the large, and now, ominous looking dark red building opposite.

The storm raged in the sky above as the rain poured down relentlessly, soaking them through their clothes to their skin.

"Are you sure you want to do this?" Thomas asked.

"This is where it began," Rebecca said.

She turned to look at Jimmy.

"Are you okay with this?" she asked.

Jimmy nodded as he stared at the building, then turned to her, "Let's do it," he said.

Rebecca smiled at him, then the three of them walked across the road from the park and entered the building.

"Not locked?" Thomas said, surprised.

"Why would it be?" Rebecca said, glancing at him.

They remained still in the entrance hall, listening.

"Maybe no one's here," Thomas said, looking around.

"No, they're here," Rebecca said.

She pointed to the left, "This way!"

Both Jimmy and Thomas followed after her as she led them to a corridor and along to Dr. Schultz's office. They went inside.

The office was empty. Papers lay on the desk arranged in small piles. Rebecca looked through them but saw nothing of interest.

"What are you looking for?" Thomas asked.

"I don't know," Rebecca said, "something."

"Try the computer," Thomas said. "Anything of interest will be on the computer."

Rebecca glanced across at him, "I'd rather not!" she said.

Both Jimmy and Thomas went around the room studying the photos on the walls.

"There's something strange about these photos," Jimmy said.

Thomas looked at him, "What?" he asked.

Jimmy studied one photo of the doctor closely. Dr. Schultz was standing outside a hospital with a few other people smiling.

"Look at the date," Jimmy said.

Thomas looked at the date, "Thirty years ago, so?"

"The doctor hasn't aged a bit since then," Jimmy said.

Rebecca came over to look at the photo.

"You're right!" she said, studying the photo closely.

Suddenly, they heard a noise. Each of them glanced upwards.

"Upstairs!" Thomas said.

They left the office and ran along the corridor to the stairs. Thomas bounded up the stairs two at a time and was the first to reach the landing on the first floor. He ran forward through the swing doors and stopped. He saw rows of beds the length of a long room on both sides, but nobody was there. Rebecca and Jimmy came running in and stopped behind him.

"They're gone," Rebecca said, looking at the rows of empty beds. "They're all gone."

They heard the noise again at the far end of the room beyond another pair of swing doors.

Rebecca glanced at Thomas, "Did I tell you that this place is haunted?" she said.

Thomas looked at her, "You 'are' kidding! Right?"

"Actually," Jimmy said beside him, "she's not."

Thomas went over to a nearby bed and grabbed a walking stick which was leaning against it. He held it up in front of him as if he were holding a club.

"We'd better get armed!" he said.

Jimmy nodded. He looked around, went over to different bed and grabbed another walking stick. Rebecca remained still, staring towards the swing doors at the far end of the long room.

Thomas looked at her, "You'd better grab something to fight with," he said.

Rebecca took no notice of him as she continued staring towards the doors.

"It's him." she said softly. "It's the ghost ... I feel it."

She moved forward and started to walk along the long room towards the swing doors.

"Rebecca?" Jimmy said, watching her go.

He followed after her, gripping the walking stick tightly in his hands. Thomas turned to look behind them, then followed them along the room.

Rebecca reached the swing doors. She stopped, hesitated, then pushed them open.

A faint glow appeared in front of her, then she saw the little boy she had seen before standing in the corridor front of her and staring directly into her eyes. A light seemed to glow around him. Jimmy and Thomas came through the swing doors behind her and entered the corridor. They stopped in their tracks as they saw the little boy.

"Wha ... what is it?" Thomas said, staring wide-eyed at the little boy standing in front of them. "Is ... is this ... the ghost?"

Neither Rebecca nor Jimmy answered.

They remained still and watched as the little boy pointed up the staircase to his left. He seemed to speak, to say something, but no words came out of his mouth.

Rebecca nodded, "I understand," she said.

Thomas looked at her, "What? You ... you understood? What... what did it say?" he asked, staring at her in a mixture of surprise and complete shock.

"He said we must go upstairs," Jimmy said, turning towards Thomas. "To the blue room."

Thomas looked at him, then turned back to the boy and gasped in shock as the little boy started to disappear in front of them.

"Let's go!" Rebecca said, turning towards the staircase.

Jimmy followed her, but Thomas remained still for a moment, staring at the now empty space where the little boy had been standing.

"Come on!" Jimmy called back to him, going up the staircase.

Thomas seemed to jerk as if the sound of Jimmy's voice had brought him out of a trance-like state. He turned and quickly ran up the staircase behind Jimmy.

At the top, they reached another corridor and ran along it to a blue door further down on the left.

Rebecca stood in front of the door staring at the door's handle and hesitating before reaching out to grasp it. She gripped the handle tightly, then slowly turned it and pushed the door open. The door creaked in the silence as it opened inwards. The room inside was dimly lit with a red light. The three of them stepped forward and entered.

And then they saw them.

CHAPTER 34

They moved further into the room, gazing down in horror at the rows of dead bodies, some of them piled up on either side. They were bodies of young children, boys and girls, their lifeless eyes staring up in a fixed and frozen stare of total fear, as if they had seen something horrible before they were killed.

Thomas held his stomach and doubled over, retching and vomiting. Rebecca, who was moving forward and looking at the bodies with wide horror-filled eyes, suddenly stopped and stared down at the body of one little boy in particular. Slowly, she stepped towards him followed by Jimmy who was also staring down at the little boy's body. They both recognized it as the body of the little boy they had previously seen, the little boy ghost.

"Why? Why?' Thomas said from behind them, his voice broken with emotion as he spoke. "Why kill ... all these children?"

Tears ran down his face as he stared at the surrounding dead bodies bathed in the room's red light.

"Because they could see them," Rebecca said quietly, her voice filled with sadness. "They could see them, see them for what they really are, long before adults could."

"It wasn't necessary," Jimmy said, standing beside Rebecca and staring down at the little boy's body. "Adults never believe what children say anyway."

Rebecca knelt down and gently touched the dead little boy's face.

"He tried to tell us," she said. "He came back to try to warn us, to help us."

"The ... the monsters!" Jimmy shouted, losing his calm.

He gripped the walking stick firmly in his hand, then turned and strode back towards the door.

"Jimmy!" Rebecca called, turning to him.

Jimmy had almost reached the door, when suddenly it opened.

Jimmy stopped in his tracks as Tony appeared in the open doorway staring towards him. An unpleasant grin stretched across Tony's face, then slowly, his body began to change. His fingers grew longer and his body seemed to grow bigger, then his skin began to peel away to reveal a demon-like monster which now stared at Jimmy with bright red eyes. The monster opened its mouth and Jimmy saw its sharp teeth as a low growl came from its throat.

Then the monster lunged forward.

"Jimmy!" Rebecca cried out.

But the monster didn't reach Jimmy, instead, Thomas ran forward from Jimmy's right, swinging the walking stick in his hands like a club as he did so.

The monster fell back onto the floor in pain growling loudly as the stick hit it squarely on the nose.

"Go!" Thomas yelled. "Get out of here!"

"Thomas! No!" Rebecca cried out as the monster now stood up, ready to lunge towards him.

"Go!' Thomas cried out once more, holding the stick ready to hit the monster again.

Both Jimmy and Rebecca ran past him to the door as the monster lunged towards Thomas, growling loudly and ready to tear him apart with its claws.

Rebecca and Jimmy ran outside and as they did the door slammed shut behind them. Rebecca turned back towards the closed door shouting.

"Thomas! Thomas!"

Behind the door they heard Thomas' screams coming from inside the room.

"My God!" Rebecca said, stepping back and staring at the closed door.

"Look!" Jimmy said, grabbing Rebecca's arm and pointing further along the corridor.

The ghost-boy was standing there again, his face pale white as he stood pointing upwards towards the nearby staircase.

"Come on!" Jimmy cried out, pulling on Rebecca's hand.

The boy once more disappeared as they reached him. They passed the spot where he had been standing and turned to run up the staircase as Thomas' screams still sounded loudly behind them.

*

On the floor above, they found themselves in the strange lopsided corridor they had run along previously sometime ago. They went along it, leaning to the side as they did so, then pushed through the swing doors at the end and saw the ghost-boy again pointing towards a door on the right. Once again, the boy disappeared as they reached him. Jimmy hesitated, standing in front of the door, then turned the door's handle. The door opened inwards and both Jimmy and Rebecca stood in the open doorway looking into the room. The room was totally black, the walls, the ceiling, the floor, everything was black. In one corner, a small red light shone from a fixture in the wall. As they entered, a large eye appeared on the wall to their left. It stared at them.

"This reminds me of ..." Rebecca began to say.

"The King's room," Jimmy said, finishing Rebecca's sentence for her, as he looked at the large eye.

They glanced around, then suddenly they made out a large black box lying in one corner on the far side of the room. They both moved forward, walking across the room towards the box and knelt down in front of it. Slowly, Rebecca reached forward and lifted the lid. A swirling storm with black clouds, flashes of lightning and sounds of booming thunder appeared inside.

"Ah! I see you've found my box!" a voice said from behind them.

Both Rebecca and Jimmy spun round to see Dr. Schultz and Miss Wong standing in the open doorway and staring down at them. Hanging from around Dr. Schutz's neck, Rebecca and Jimmy saw a golden key.

CHAPTER 35

Both Dr. Schultz and Miss Wong entered the room slowly, staring at Rebecca and Jimmy, with strange piercing eyes.

The world has changed, has it not?" Dr. Schultz said. "My master, he now controls it. He has been awaiting this day for a long time!"

"Your master? You mean the Darkness?" Rebecca said. "That pathetic creature in the other world?"

Dr. Schultz stopped moving forward. He remained perfectly still, his eyes fixed on her.

"The one you met in that world, he was not the master. He serves the master, just like I do! The master is no pathetic creature! He is all power-ful! A God! A God who desires to be worshipped and admired! And to those who serve him, he bestows gifts! Power! Control of worlds in his name! And I ... I will be the controller of 'this' world!"

Dr. Schultz's eyes gleamed insanely as he stared down at them. "In his name ... of course!" he added.

Both Rebecca and Jimmy remained still, staring up at him.

"So, in other words, you're just a puppet, aren't you?" Rebecca said, after a moment's silence.

The doctor's eyes widened, an angry sneer appeared on his lips as an animal-like growl came from him.

"A puppet?" he repeated angrily. "I am much more than a mere puppet! Choose your words carefully young lady! You 'will' be obedient! Unless your prefer torture, of course! I am sure Miss Wong here would love to have you tied down on one of our racks! She finds torture a great amusement! Her methods of torture can be … quite persuasive! Mind-changing! She will have you begging in …!"

"Why kill the children?" Jimmy asked, trying to change the subject. "The homeless?"

Dr. Schultz regarded him for a moment, then seemed to regain his calm a little, "There are those who see us, see us for what we really are, just like the children! The homeless … and others! Those, we cannot control! Those, just like you and your friend! But soon, all those we cannot con-trol … will die! Just as you and your friend are going to die!"

Then he grinned an insane-looking grin as he stared at them.

"But first … I believe Miss Wong deserves her 'amusement', don't you?"

Both Jimmy and Rebecca saw a smile come onto Miss Wong's lips.

The doctor growled, and then his body began to change as he started to transform himself into the demon-like monster they had previously seen. Miss Wong, standing behind him, also began to transform herself, and within seconds, two demon-like monsters stood in front of both Rebecca and Jimmy, growling savagely.

"What do we do?" Jimmy said to Rebecca.

They both took a step backwards as the two demons moved towards them, continuing to growl at them like savage beasts. They stared at the demons' red glowing eyes, their sharp pointed teeth and the claws on their long fingers.

"We must get the key!" Rebecca said urgently, staring at the key hanging from around, what was once, Dr. Schultz's neck.

"Stay behind me!" Jimmy said, moving in front of Rebecca.

"Jimmy! No!" Rebecca shouted.

Suddenly, Jimmy let out a wild cry, raising the stick he was holding, and charged towards both demons. He hit the demon that had once been the doctor in the stomach, but the blow had little effect. The demon growled louder and picked Jimmy up effortlessly off the floor. Jimmy cried out hanging suspended above the floor in the demon's grip and trying to kick towards it, while the other demon, who had once been Miss Wong, now came forward, growling towards Rebecca.

The light! Rebecca thought, remembering what was written in the book. Show no fear! Vanquish them with light!

"I have no fear of you!" Rebecca said, staring up at the demon.

The words seemed to make the demon pause in front of her. Then suddenly, Rebecca dropped down on to her knees, clasped her hands together, and began to pray.

"Please dear God!" Rebecca said. "Deliver us from this evil! Please bring light into this world! Please ...!" and then she began saying the words under her breath.

The demon-like creature now towered above her, opening its hands with its pointed claws about to strike her. It paused, staring down at Rebecca as she prayed silently on the floor, then growled loudly and was about to hit her when something strange happened. A light suddenly appeared. It came from within Rebecca's body, and then it started to surround her. The light grew brighter, growing in intensity, brighter and brighter, and then suddenly, the demon who had been about to strike her staggered back and cried out with an ear-splitting scream as the light seemed to shoot up from Rebecca and into it. A bright burning fire now engulfed the creature's whole body, the flames rising high as the creature twisted and turned and staggered back trying to escape the all consuming flames. And then, a moment later, the demon seemed to explode and disappear, and all that was left on the floor in front of Rebecca was now a pile of ash. The demon, who had once been the doctor, threw the screaming Jimmy effortlessly across the room and turned to gaze down at the ash on the floor. It growled loudly, then looked at Rebecca and the glowing bright light surrounding her.

Rebecca remained kneeling, staring up at it.

"I am not afraid of you," she said, and then bowed her head and continued her prayer.

The demon growled again angrily, moving towards her. It was about to strike her when suddenly it stopped as if it had somehow been paralyzed. As Rebecca continued to pray, a blinding light once again rose from her and then shot towards the demon, hitting it. The demon screamed loudly and then burst into flames. It turned away, twisting and turning and screaming wildly as it staggered across the room trying to escape the flames which now engulfed it. Then suddenly, it exploded and disappeared, leaving another pile of ash on the floor.

Jimmy leaned up from where he had fallen, first gazing down at the ash on the floor and then staring across at Rebecca, his mouth open in both surprise and shock as Rebecca remained kneeling, her eyes closed, looking serene and bathed in a brilliant white light. As Jimmy watched, the light surrounding Rebecca slowly started to disappear, and then it was gone. Rebecca opened her eyes.

"What ... what just happened?" Jimmy asked, continuing to stare at her in amazement.

Rebecca looked at the ash on the floor in front of her, and then at Jimmy.

"I prayed," she said. "I prayed for help. I ... I prayed for God to help us."

CHAPTER 36

Rebecca leaned forward looking at the two piles of ash in front of her.

"How ... how did you know that would work?" Jimmy asked, staring across at her.

"I didn't," Rebecca said. "But ... I remembered what it said in the book about the light. I realized that the doctor somehow brought the Darkness into this world, and if he could bring darkness, then maybe, someone could bring light."

She stood up and went over to the pile of ash that had once been the doctor. She gazed down at it, then knelt beside it and pushed the ash aside with her hand.

"What are you doing?" Jimmy asked, now getting up onto his feet and watching her curiously.

Suddenly, Rebecca saw the key just under the ash and picked it up. She turned to him with a smile and held the key up in front of her.

"We have the key!" she said.

Rebecca stood up and went back over to the box. Jimmy remained still, staring down at the two piles of ash.

"That ... that light which came from you," Jimmy said, as Rebecca knelt down in front of the box holding the key, "are you ... religious?" he asked, now turning to look at her.

"I believe in God," Rebecca said, looking back at him. "If there is evil, then there must be good. And if evil resides in darkness, what is stronger than darkness?" she asked.

"Light," Jimmy answered.

Rebecca nodded, "Right," she said.

She gazed down at the key in her hand, "This world has become so dark, and a dark place needs light. That is the light that the book was talking about. And yes, to your question, I now believe in God more than ever before." She turned back to look at him, "I ... I felt something Jimmy, when that light surrounded me. I felt ... peace, an indescribable peace! It was like ... I was floating."

Jimmy remained still, staring down at her, then nodded. Rebecca glanced back down at the key in her hand, then reached forward and placed it into the lock. She paused, then turned it and heard a 'click' as it locked the box.

Jimmy came over and crouched down beside her, "Is that it?" he asked. "Just ... lock the box?"

Rebecca stared down at the box which was now locked, "I ... I hope so." she said.

She looked at him, "If this works … this must never be opened again."

Jimmy nodded, "Yes," he agreed.

At first, nothing happened, then suddenly, the black room in which they were, began to change. The blackness slowly began to disappear, and the once dark room became lighter, brighter. Both Rebecca and Jimmy gazed around at the transformation in open-mouthed wonder. They glanced back down at the box on the floor in front of them and saw that it was now changing colour to a brilliant bright blue.

Rebecca raised her head, "Do you hear that?" she said.

Jimmy looked at her.

"What?" he asked.

"The thunder's stopped," she said. "There's no more storm."

They both stood up.

"Let's go see!" Rebecca said, turning and running across the room to the door. Outside, the corridor which had previously seemed strange now looked normal. Rebecca ran along it and into one of the rooms with a window. She ran over to the window, opened it and looked outside.

The sun was shining brightly above in a beautiful blue sky, and in the park opposite, birds were singing and flying happily from tree to tree. Jimmy joined her and gazed out of the window at the beautiful sunny day outside. He smiled, looking at the world as if he were seeing it for the first time.

"What do we do now?" he asked.

Rebecca looked at him.

"Now we go back and get Ruth and Ellie," she said.

CHAPTER 37

"It's still here," Jimmy said, standing in the room beside Rebecca.

They both stood, staring in front of them at the dark swirling mass shaped like a tunnel which continued to turn relentlessly.

"Why doesn't it disappear?" Jimmy asked.

"There's still a corridor to the other world somehow," Rebecca said. "It doesn't matter how. Right now, I just want to get Ruth and Ellie back safely."

"So ... we go through it again?" Jimmy said, staring at the swirling dark tunnel in front of them.

Rebecca looked at him, "You ... you don't have to come," she said. "They're my friends. You can stay here."

Jimmy turned to her, "And let you go alone?" he said, amazed at her suggestion. "There's no way I'm letting you go back for Ruth and Ellie alone!"

He raised a baseball bat he'd found in one of the rooms, "I'm ready if you are!"

Rebecca smiled back him.

"Thanks," she said.

She turned to look once again at the dark tunnel, then took a deep breath, "Here goes!" she said.

She ran forward, followed by Jimmy, and together they leapt into the swirling mass of darkness.

They seemed to be falling uncontrollably like they had before, with a feeling of weightlessness. Time passed as they continued to fall, seconds, minutes, they couldn't be sure, and then they fell from the swirling dark tunnel and landed on the ground beneath it, rolling. Jimmy lay still breathing heavily and glanced across to Rebecca who was lying on the wet grass beside him. Once again, it was pouring with rain.

"You okay?" he asked.

Rebecca leaned up, nodding, "I'm okay," she said. "You?"

Jimmy pushed himself up onto his feet, "Okay," he said. "I'm never going to get used to that thing!"

"Let's hope we won't have to," Rebecca said, standing up beside him.

Together they looked up at the black rolling clouds above them. Lightning flashed across the dark storm-filled sky and thunder boomed and rumbled loudly.

"Well ..." Jimmy said, "we're back!"

Rebecca sighed, studying the sky, then looked at Jimmy.

"Okay, let's go," she said, pointing the way across the landscape towards the castle.

*

As they walked in the pouring rain across the wet grassy landscape, the lightning in the sky above crashed down towards them as if it were alive. They stopped as a lightning bolt hit a tree on the edge of the large field to their left setting fire to it, and then another hit a tree farther away to their right.

"Do you get the feeling someone's trying to tell us something?" Jimmy said to Rebecca.

Rebecca pointed in front of her.

"Look!" she said.

Jimmy looked to where she was pointing and saw the large triangular gate with its steps leading up to what looked like a screen showing an image of another world on the other side with a calm blue sky and beautiful rolling fields. Two creature-like guards stood on either side of the triangular gate as other guards herded a long line of people through the field towards it. Both Rebecca and Jimmy stared at the scene in front of them.

"Ruth!" Rebecca cried out, suddenly seeing her friend in the line of people being herded towards the gate.

"There's Sev!" Jimmy said, pointing towards the small people moving slowly forward in the long line. "And Roe ... and the King!"

"They're going to be taken into the other world!" Rebecca said.

Jimmy lifted his baseball bat in front of him, "Stay here!" he said.

"Jimmy!" Rebecca called, trying to grab his arm as Jimmy ran forward, but she was too late. He ran across the field towards the long line of people and the guards, gripping the baseball bat tightly in his hands like a club. As he neared them, he started screaming loudly. The guards turned, surprised to see him running towards them. Before they could react, he knocked two of the guards to the ground before running towards a third. The third guard tried to defend himself with his spear-like weapon but Jimmy managed to knock it out of the way and hit the guard to the ground. Other guards now appeared shouting and running towards him.

Jimmy glanced at the long line of people.

"Fight back! Fight back!" he shouted to them.

Then he noticed their eyes which were glazed as if they were in some kind of a trance.

At first, the people merely stared at him, watching as Jimmy began to fight the attacking guards, then Jimmy saw a light coming from across the field where he'd left Rebecca. The light seemed to hit the King, making him cry out, then his eyes changed and he now became normal and looked around to see what was happening. The light then hit other people in the long line, bringing each one back to their senses and back to normal. The King saw the guards attacking Jimmy and cried out for his people to run forward and join in the fighting. Jimmy now found himself fighting the guards beside the King who had been able to pick up one of the guard's fallen spear-like weapon. The two guards who had been standing on the steps beside the triangular gateway to another world ran forward and down the steps to join in the fight. Although the King's people were small, there were more of them than there were guards, and soon the guards were overwhelmed and beaten. Jimmy grinned towards Rebecca who was still standing on the other side of the field with a strong white light radiating around her, and then he turned and saw Ruth. Her eyes were remained glazed and she was still walking up the steps towards the triangular gate.

"No!" Jimmy shouted.

He ran forward and up the steps just as Ruth disappeared inside the gate. He reached the gate, hesitated as he stood in front of the screen-like image of a beautiful world on the other side, and then he entered. As he passed through the gate, he found himself in another world, but unlike the image outside, this world was not beautiful. He froze, staring at the landscape in front of him. It was red, everything was covered in red, as if someone had covered the whole landscape and everything in it in blood. The landscape in front of him was desolate, like a huge wasteland after an incredibly destructive war. Here and there he saw volcano's erupting, spewing out bright red lava. He heard people, hundreds of them, crying and wailing in pain. And then he saw them. Their heads and bodies seemed to be stuck in bizarre looking nightmarish structures which rose from the ground all around him. He gazed around with horror-filled eyes at the nightmarish scenery surrounding him, and then he saw Ruth. Blood was running down her body as she was walking slowly away from him towards one of the strange and twisted nightmarish looking structures which held more people who were stuck inside and who were crying, sobbing and wailing incessantly.

"Ruth!" Jimmy cried out.

Ruth suddenly stopped walking and slowly turned to face him. Her eyes were glazed as she seemed to stare through him.

Suddenly, a voice spoke from nowhere. It was a deep, menacing booming voice which shook the ground beneath Jimmy as it spoke.

"YOU CANNOT HAVE HER!" it boomed out loudly.

Jimmy stared around him, his heart beating faster in fear at the sound of the voice.

"Leave her!" he managed to shout. "Leave her alone!"

The voice laughed.

There was no humour in the laughter, only the sound of menace, of evil in its purest form.

"SHE IS MINE!" the voice boomed out again..

Jimmy stared at Ruth who remained still, staring back at him with glazed trance-like eyes.

"No!" Jimmy said, shaking his head. "No! Leave her alone! Leave her alone!"

The voice laughed again, its laughter sounding as if it were all around him.

Ruth turned and once again began walking towards the nightmarish looking structure.

Jimmy ran forward and grabbed her hand to stop her. Suddenly, his feet seemed to be stuck in the ground. He looked down and saw a red sticky substance coming out of the ground, climbing up and covering his feet and now rising slowly up his legs towards his body.

"Jimmy!"

He heard the voice behind him, calling his name.

"Jimmy!"

It was Rebecca's voice.

The red sticky substance had now reached his waist and was continuing to move up him. Jimmy wanted to turn, to look back, but he couldn't. Instead, he remained staring towards Ruth, still gripping onto her hand tightly, not daring to let go. Suddenly, he noticed a light appear around him, covering him. The light moved forward and now also began to engulf Ruth in front of him. Jimmy glanced down and saw the red sticky substance now beginning to leave his body and sink back into the ground. He looked up and saw the glazed trance-like stare leave Ruth's eyes. She blinked and gazed around, then she screamed.

"NO!" boomed the voice loudly, shaking the ground beneath their feet.

Jimmy felt himself rising. He kept hold on Ruth's hand, gripping it tightly as he saw that she too was rising with him, both of them surrounded by a bright light. Ruth gazed around, her eyes wide in fear as she continued screaming. And then they were floating, floating back towards the strange triangular gate they had passed through.

"NOOOO!" the voice boomed again, as lightning flashed and thunder crashed, surrounding them and seeming to come from nowhere.

And then the light transported them back through the gate, out of the macabre and sinister blood red world, and they found themselves standing once again in front of the triangular gate showing a beautiful image into the other world they had just left. The light disappeared around them and Ruth stopped screaming and leapt towards Jimmy throwing her arms around him and squeezing him tightly.

"Thank you! Thank you! Thank you!" she said, not wanting to let go of him.

Jimmy saw Rebecca standing nearby completely surrounded in a glowing bright light. Slowly, the light began to fade and then it disappeared.

"Thank you," he said towards her.

Rebecca smiled at him and looked at Ruth who remained hugging Jimmy tightly in her arms. The King came over to her followed by Sev and Roe.

"Thank you!" the King said, gazing into her eyes. He leaned forward and hugged her, as did Sev and Roe.

"We are in your debt again!" the King said. "Once again I owe you my life, and the lives of my people!" He looked at Jimmy, "And you ... you fight like a great warrior!" he said.

Jimmy looked down, embarrassed by the King's words.

The King turned back to Rebecca, "You have a great magic!" he said. "That light!"

Ruth shook her head, "No, it ... it's not magic. It's ... something ... something we call faith."

The King gazed at her for a moment.

"Faith?" he repeated.

Rebecca nodded, "Yes."

The King shrugged, "Well, whatever you call it, it is a strong magic!"

Ruth turned to look back at her friend.

"Rebecca!" she said. "Oh my God! It was so ...!"

Rebecca moved over to her and placed her arms around her, "It's over now," she said, hugging Ruth tightly. "It's over."

Tears were running down Ruth's face as she leaned back to look at her friend, then she turned and reached out her hand towards Jimmy. She grasped his hand and held onto it tightly.

"You ... you're my hero!" she said, her eyes filled with tears as she gazed at him.

Jimmy seemed embarrassed as he looked back at her feeling Ruth's hand continuing to squeeze his tightly.

"Just ... just glad you're safe," he said, glancing down away from her eyes.

Rebecca turned back to the King, "King ... by the way ... what is your name?"

The King shrugged, "Just King," he answered.

He glanced up at the rain, beating at his face, "Let us find shelter," he said. "There is a cavern not far from here."

Rebecca nodded, "Good idea," she agreed.

*

Rebecca and Jimmy followed the King and his people who led them out of the pouring rain and into yet another secret cavern. On the way, Ruth refused to let go of Jimmy's hand, saying that she felt safe holding onto to it. Jimmy felt embarrassed as she continued to grip his hand tightly in hers.

In the cavern, the small people quickly built several fires for everyone to huddle around and dry themselves.

"What of my friend, Tol?" Roe asked, looking at Rebecca.

Rebecca glanced down, "I ... I don't know. We were separated. I thought if he got away, he'd ... come back."

Roe shook his head sadly, "He didn't come back," he said.

"I'm sorry," Rebecca said, looking at him.

"Maybe ... he will come back later, "Sev said, looking at Rebecca with a hopeful smile.

"I ... I hope so," Rebecca said, looking back at her.

As they sat around the fire, Rebecca glanced at the King

"In our world, we saw another box. And there was a doctor who transformed himself into a ... a demon-like monster, just like the Darkness in your world."

"Yes ... I was afraid of that," the King said. "I believe these ... boxes, are in every world. That the Darkness preys on the weak, those who are in need of something more than they have. The Darkness makes promises ... and those ... those who follow him, are transformed into demons. They become his servants, but what they really don't understand is ... they become his slaves. In your world, a doctor became the Darkness, and in my world ... it was my brother."

Rebecca, Jimmy and Ruth stared at him.

"Your ... brother?" Jimmy asked

The King looked at him, then nodded.

"My brother Erin," he said. "Erin was always jealous of me. I was King, he was not." The king glanced down sadly, then shrugged, "I didn't understand how deeply he resented me, until one day, I heard that he has begun using black magic. In this world, we use magic, but we only use it for good. Black magic is bad, evil. Erin was soon drawn towards it, towards its power. He wanted to be King, he wanted to be tall, he wanted to be admired, he wanted ... everything, everything he didn't have, even ... my Queen." He paused, gazing into the fire. "She ... she perished saving my life when Erin took power, using the box given to him by the Darkness, the 'real' Darkness."

"So ... the Darkness in this world is ... is your brother!" Rebecca said.

The King nodded sadly.

Jimmy leaned forward, staring at him, "And ... the 'real' Darkness?" he said. "He is in that world beyond the triangular gate?"

The King looked at him.

"Yes," he answered. "That is ... yes and no. In fact, he is everywhere, watching, waiting. I believe he is in all worlds, but no one really sees him. Those creatures who work for my brother, they were our own people. They were taken into the 'Never' world, the world ruled by the 'true' Darkness, and when they returned, they were transformed. Transformed into ... creatures, demons ..."

"We can stop them!" Rebecca said. "Just like I did in my world with the doctor, we can stop them!"

The King studied her.

"Will this ... power you have ... this ... this light, will it ... will it kill my brother?"

Rebecca stared at him, then lowered her head and nodded, "Yes," she said.

Tears came into the king's eyes as he glanced down.

"Then ... it must be so," he said sadly.

He stood up.

"Come! Let us not delay! We must finish this! We must finish this now!"

The King turned to look down at Roe who was sitting nearby.

"Gather everyone!" the King said. "The time for waiting is no longer!"

CHAPTER 38

The strange looking creature kneeling down in front of the Darkness who was sitting on the throne was visibly shaking.

"Master!" he said, in a trembling voice, obviously filled with fear. "We ... we do not know what happened, how ... how it happened ..."

The Darkness stared down at him, leaning forward from the throne.

"You say the guards were killed?" the Darkness said in a deeply threatening voice.

The creature nodded, not daring to look up at the Darkness who was staring down at him, his eyes blazing red.

"Ye ... yes master! All of them!"

"And the gateway into the other world?" the Darkness said.

"It ... it is intact master!" the creature said.

The Darkness breathed heavily, then sat back in the throne.

"Send out the riders!" he said. "Find them! and bring the King to me!"

The creature bowed fearfully, "Yes! ... Yes master!" he said, then he turned and ran across the Great Hall towards the huge open doors.

The Darkness watched him depart, then sat thoughtfully staring in front of him.

*

The King exited the secret passage followed by Rebecca, Jimmy and Ruth and the rest of his people. They went across the large room, which was once a library, to the door on the far side and peered out into the dimly-lit corridor.

"My people will take care of the demon creatures," the King said, looking at Rebecca. "We will go to the Great Hall. My brother will surely be there, he likes to sit on my throne."

"What about our friend?" Jimmy asked. "Ellie."

She is probably in a dungeon," the king said. "Or in the torture chamber."

Jimmy looked at Rebecca, "You see to the King's brother," he said. "Get the key! I'll find Ellie."

Ruth squeezed Jimmy's hand as she stood beside him, "'We'll' find Ellie!" she said. "Together!"

Jimmy looked into her eyes, then shook his head, "It's too dangerous," he said. "You'd be safer with the others, with Rebecca."

"No," Ruth said, looking back into Jimmy's eyes, "I ... I feel safe with you."

Jimmy glanced down, once again embarrassed, "It was Rebecca who saved you, not me," he said. "She saved us both! You'll be safer with her, believe me."

Ruth shook her head, still gazing into his eyes and gripping his hand tightly, "I'm coming with you," she said.

Rebecca studied the way Ruth was looking at Jimmy and smiled, then she looked at Jimmy, "Take good care of her," she said. "And find Ellie!"

Jimmy hesitated, then nodded, "I will," he said. "Be careful."

The King turned and looked at four of his men, "Go with them," he ordered. "Show them the way to the dungeons."

The four men nodded.

"I've been there before," Jimmy said, looking at him.

"I know," the King said with a smile. "Just in case you get lost."

The four small men pushed past both Jimmy and Ruth and stepped out into the corridor.

"This way," one of the men said, glancing back to Jimmy and pointing to the left.

Jimmy shrugged, "Okay!" he said, looking down at the little man.

He glanced at Rebecca, nodded farewell, then stepped out into the corridor with Ruth still grasping onto his hand tightly.

Rebecca watched them go.

The King glanced at her, "Are you ready?" he asked.

Rebecca looked back at both Sev and Rue who were standing behind her, then back at the King and nodded, "I'm ready," she said.

*

In the torture chamber far below, Krawl was standing in front of Ellie who was chained naked to the wall.

He studied her beauty as she cried, sobbing and begging for him to release her.

"Please!" Ellie begged. "Please! Le ... let me go! Please! I ... I beg you! Please!"

Krawl moved towards her and reached out a hand to caress her body. Ellie screamed at the touch of his hand and jerked in her bonds.

"No! No! Please! Please!"

But krawl smiled and continued to touch her.

"When I was normal," he said, "no girl would even look at me. I was always cast aside, like some pathetic creature! And now ... now I can have any girl I want. And what I want ... is you!"

Ellie screamed again loudly, unable to avoid his touch.

"Such ... perfection!" Krawl said, as he admired Ellie's body. "Such beauty!"

Krawl grinned, looking into Ellie's eyes, "I will have ... so much fun with you!" he said. "So much fun!"

Ellie screamed again seeing Krawl's sharp pointed teeth as he grinned at her. Then he moved closer. Ellie gasped uncontrollably, staring with wide fear-filled eyes at him as her body jerked to his touch..

"So sensitive!" Krawl whispered. "Such perfection!"

*

Jimmy, Ruth and the four small men reached the dungeons and had begun to look inside some of the cells when they heard Ellie scream.

"Ellie!" Jimmy cried out, looking along the dungeon's dimly-lit corridor towards the torture chamber. He ran forward with Ruth behind him who was still holding tightly onto Jimmy's hand. Jimmy ran as fast as he could along the corridor pulling Ruth behind him and followed by the King's men.

He reached the torture chamber and pushed on the door. It was unlocked. The door creaked open and he went inside quickly, and then he stopped, horrified at what he saw. Krawl, who was crouching down and licking at Ellie's bound body with an extremely long tongue as she screamed and bucked helplessly in her bonds, turned to look at him. Slowly, Krawl stood up and turned to face him as Jimmy remained still staring across at both him and Ellie.

Krawl grinned towards him, showing his sharp pointed teeth. Jimmy felt Ruth's hand grip his even tighter as she took a step back in fear of the red skinned demon. Suddenly Jimmy yelled, an anger raging through him, as he let go of Ruth's hand and ran forward brandishing the baseball bat he now gripped tightly in both hands. Krawl raised a hand towards him and the next thing Jimmy knew he was flying back across the torture chamber. He hit the far wall and cried out, then fell unconscious to the floor.

"Jimmy!" Ruth cried out, staring towards him.

The King's men ran forward towards Krawl shouting as Ruth turned to look at the red skinned demon who was now grinning at them almost insanely. Ruth backed away fearfully and hid behind a pile of old torture devices. She watched as krawl pointed his hand towards them and the men fell back across the chamber crying out. One of them landed just nearby where Ruth was hiding and she screamed as she saw him land on a sharp instrument. She raised her hand to her mouth in horror as she saw blood pouring out of the man's chest from the sharp pointed device that had passed straight through him. Ruth heard Krawl laughing and turned to see him holding one small man suspended in mid-air with an invisible power that seemed to come from Krawl's hand as he directed it up towards the man. Krawl jerked his hand quickly to the right and the man flew across the chamber, screaming and as he went, and hit the far wall with a force which crushed the man's head. The man fell lifeless to the ground and Ruth remained still with her hand covering her mouth trying to stop herself from screaming as she hid behind the device keeping her out of sight.

She glanced back over to Jimmy, wanting to run over to him, but was afraid of what the demon would do to her if she did so.

The other two men who had fallen back onto the floor now stood up staring towards Krawl. Krawl grinned, looking at them, and then raised his hand. The man in front suddenly shot upwards, hit the ceiling with a force, and then fell back down to the floor dead. The last remaining man let out an angry yell and charged towards Krawl running as fast as he could. Krawl merely watched him, and then just before the man could reach him, he pointed his hand towards the man and the man rose up from the ground to hover in mid-air. Krawl continued to grin as he watched him, then the man spat towards him. Krawl's grin turned into a snarl. He glanced to his right and saw a club-like instrument of torture with spikes sticking out of it. He raised his other hand and the instrument rose as if by itself up from the ground. He looked back at the man suspended in mid-air in front of him, then did something with the hand which held him up in its power. The man gasped, his eyes widening as he glanced down at his legs which were now spreading out beneath him as if they had a will of their own. The man now glanced at the instrument of torture with the spikes which hovered in the air to his left. His eyes widened in fear as he realized what Krawl was about to do, and then he screamed as the instrument flew across the chamber and then embedded itself into the man's body between his widely extended legs. The man's loud screams slowly became an uncontrolled gurgle as his body jerked and blood gushed down from between his legs and onto the floor beneath him. Krawl dropped his hands and watched as the man fell lifeless to the floor in front of him. He giggled, the he turned back to Ellie who was trembling uncontrollably and staring down at the man's dead body with wide terror-filled eyes.

"Now," krawl said looking at her with a grin, "where were we my beauty?"

CHAPTER 39

As the King, Rebecca and the others approached the Great Hall, at least thirty creatures appeared in the corridor in front of them.

"Forward!" the King shouted without hesitation, and started yelling and charging towards the creatures followed by his people. The king raised his right hand as he ran forward and a yellow light shot out of his hand to hit the creatures in front. Three of the creatures cried out and fell back and then the two sides clashed. Both the creatures and the King's people began fighting and shouting wildly. Rebecca managed to push one creature out of the way as he lunged towards her. She heard the king shouting and turned to see him running towards the two huge doors which led to the Great Hall. She pushed her way through the fighting mass trying to get over to him, avoiding two more creatures who lunged forward in her direction. A creature came from her left and was about to hit her when Roe ran forward to block him. Rebecca continued, pushing her way through the fighting mass and avoiding other attacks, before finally reaching the King who was fighting off another creature outside the two huge doors. Rebecca ran at the creature pushing him with all her might and the creature stumbled back, then the king raised his hand and a bolt of yellow light hit the creature in the chest forcing him back onto the floor with a cry. The King quickly turned and pushed open the two huge doors just wide enough to pass through. The king quickly entered, followed by Rebecca, and the moment they had entered, the two huge doors closed behind them as if they had a life of their own. Inside, across the Great Hall, they saw the Darkness sitting on the throne gazing towards them.

"I have been expecting you ... my brother!" the Darkness said.

The Darkness moved back his hood and stood up, and for the first time, Rebecca could see the face of the King's brother. The face was disfigured, twisted horribly and scarred, but what was more noticeable, were the eyes that shone bright red, as if there were a light, a fire burning and shining from inside them.

*

Ruth watched, her hands shaking uncontrollably as she stared from her hiding place at what the red skinned demon was doing to Ellie. It reminded her of her own torture, and she was afraid, so afraid of being tortured like that again if she were caught. She remembered the hands, the fingers! Crawling all over her, everywhere, everywhere! And what could she do against the demon anyway? she thought. She saw what had happened to the King's men, to Jimmy. She wouldn't be able to stand it, she knew, not again, she thought, she couldn't stand to be tortured like that again! And so she continued to watch, too afraid to try to help her friend, too afraid of being caught and of being tortured once more like she had been before. As she watched in horror, Ruth occasionally glanced across with worried tear-filled eyes to where Jimmy lay unconscious.

Krawl, who was once again standing in front of Ellie, grinned and giggled as he controlled four feathers that fluttered in front of Ellie's body, tickling her. Ellie gasped, screamed and pulled with all her might at the chains holding her firmly against the wall..

Krawl laughed as he watched her writhe and jerk to the tickling sensations the feathers were forcing upon her body.

"You see?" Krawl said. "I would never harm you. Unlike my master, the Darkness. You should see what he did to some of the girls we took as slaves. They now look like hideous monsters that even I would not wish to touch. The master has a lot of … 'hate' inside him. I would never do that to you. No, I believe that beauty such as yours is too precious, too beautiful to be harmed."

He laughed again, "Do you like my little games?" he asked. "If not now, you will do, and then … and then, you will grow to like me … to love me! I will never let anyone harm you, with me, you will always be safe, always!"

He leaned forward to kiss her and Ellie cried out, jerking her head away from him. Krawl studied her for a moment, his eyes now staring at her coldly, bitterly, then he leaned forward again and roughly forced a kiss upon her as Ellie screams were muffled and her body jerked helplessly in the chains binding her firmly to the wall. After a moment, he leaned back again studying Ellie carefully as she hung from her chains gasping and sobbing with her head lowered.

"You 'will' grow to love me!" Krawl said.

He stepped back and raised his hands, and once again the feathers hovered in front of her.

"Surely, you prefer this to pain, no?" he asked.

He moved his hands, controlling the feathers as they hung in mid-air in front of her, and then he giggled as he once again began tickling her body with them, watching with a grin on his face at how Ellie bucked and writhed and gasped uncontrollably in her chains.

Suddenly, a sound from behind Krawl made him turn around. Jimmy was up and running towards him with the baseball bat gripped tightly in his hands.

"Jimmy!" Ruth cried out as she watched, happy to see him alive and yet fearing what Krawl might do to him.

Krawl just managed to raise his hand in time before Jimmy could reach him. Jimmy let out a cry and fell back once again, but this time he managed to get back up onto his feet straight away. Krawl looked towards two of the small dead men lying on the floor in front of him. He saw that they had been carrying knives. He raised his hand and the knives floating up from the floor and hovered in mid-air. Jimmy yelled angrily and came running back towards him brandishing the baseball bat like a club. Krawl moved his hand controlling the knives and then the knives flew across the chamber towards the oncoming Jimmy. Jimmy ducked as one of the knives flew past him and the other imbedded itself in the baseball bat. Jimmy stopped in his tracks and looked at the knife sticking out of the baseball bat in surprise, then he turned just in time to see the other knife flying back towards him. He managed to duck but as the knife passed him it cut his face. Jimmy cried out in pain, and then the knife turned again attacking him. Jimmy tried to protect his face but the knife cut his hands and then his arm. Jimmy screamed as he fell to his knees trying to protect himself as the knife continued to attack him, now cutting his leg. From across the chamber he heard Krawl laughing as Krawl manouvered the knife this way and that, watching Jimmy crying out and trying to protect himself. Krawl continued with a demonic-like grin, forcing the knife to cut at Jimmy as if he were playing an amusing game.

*

The king walked across the Great hall towards his brother who now stood in front of the throne staring down at him. Rebecca remained still behind the King. In the corridor outside they could hear the battle between the King's people and the demon-like creatures, but in the Great Hall itself, there was only a deathly silence.

"I can do it," Rebecca called out to the King, her voice echoing around the hall as she spoke. "I can do it now."

The king turned to look back at her.

"No, not yet!" the King said. "Please, he is still my brother."

The Darkness stared down at them curiously, as the King turned back to face him.

The Darkness seemed to smile, "Do you see how tall I am brother?" he said, holding out his arms as he spoke. "So tall ... and so powerful! For years I watched you on this throne! I hated you! You could not imagine how much I hated you my brother!"

"And that's why you turned to black magic?" the King asked. "To become tall? To take my throne? Was I not a good brother to you, Erin?"

Erin grinned showing his sharp pointed teeth, "The Darkness is good to me!" he said. "He promised me height, and I am tall! He promised me your throne, and now I have it! He promised me admiration! Girls!

And I have them all! So ... yes! I turned to black magic brother! And it serves me well!"

"The Darkness does not serve you!" the King said. "You serve 'it'! Don't you see? 'You' are merely its servant! Its slave! The Darkness makes servants of you and others like you in all worlds! Because you are weak! Because you can easily be controlled!"

"It is I who control you! You and your people! This world! I! I and no other!"

The king shook his head sadly, "I feel sorry for you," he said.

"You?" Erin cried. "You feel sorry? For me?"

He laughed.

"You fool!" Erin said. "Do not waste your sympathy on me brother! Save it for yourself! Save it for your people! For I will send you all into the 'Never' world where the Darkness commands. There, he will transform you into his creatures, and when you return ... you will obey me! Me! Do you hear brother?"

"Just like those poor creatures who serve you already?" the King said. "Those who came back from the 'Never' world grotesquely shaped like demons? Do you think they admire you? They fear you! Your kingdom is ruled by fear! I would rather die than be one of them!"

Erin's grin grew wider.

"Then die you shall brother!" he said.

Erin raised his hand, just as the King raised his own. A red beam of light shot from Erin's fingers towards the King, but the King countered with a light of his own as a beam of yellow light shot out from his hand protecting him from being hit by Erin's red light. Rebecca watched as the King fought to protect himself, but each moment that passed it seemed that his protective yellow light was weaker.

"See how powerful I am!" Erin called down to his brother, forcing the red light emitting from his fingers to push the king's yellow light back, little by little.

"Bow to me brother!" Erin called out. "Bow to me before it is too late!"

"Never!" the King said.

He grunted, being forced back by the powerful pressure of Erin's red light.

"Never!" the King cried out again, now physically sweating from his efforts as he staggered back beneath Erin's forceful strength.

"Aaagh!" the King cried out, almost falling from the force of the red light.

Rebecca, who had been watching, and who had promised to let the King speak to his brother first to try to persuade him to change, now knelt down, clasped her hands together, and began to pray.

As Erin laughed and the King grunted falling back onto the floor from the powerful red light, Rebecca prayed, whispering the words of her prayer as fast as she could.

*

Jimmy cried out in pain as the knife cut his hand and then cut into his face. He twisted and rolled on the floor crying out and trying to escape as the knife continued to lash out at him. He managed to get back up onto his knees and then froze, seeing the knife hovering just in front of him. It moved forward and now pressed itself against his throat. Jimmy gasped, feeling the blade cut into his skin. He tried to raise his hands to stop it, but he found he couldn't move them. He remained still with the knife at his throat as if her were paralyzed.

"Now, it's your turn to die!" Krawl said, cocking his head to one side with a grin.

He giggled once more and was about to move his hand when suddenly, he cried out, and then fell forward onto the floor. Jimmy glanced up and saw Ruth standing behind him holding a heavy object in her hand. The knife which had been hovering against Jimmy's throat now dropped down clattering onto the floor in front of him. Jimmy realized that he could now move. He saw Krawl kneeling up from the floor and holding the back of his head where Ruth had hit him with the heavy object. Krawl turned to look up at Ruth who now dropped the heavy object and took a frightened step back away from him. Slowly, Krawl raised his hand up towards her. Ruth stared down at him, her eyes opening wider in fear, and then suddenly, a knife struck Krawl in the chest. Krawl froze, then stared down at the knife with a surprised expression on his face. He remained still, then looked up at Jimmy who had thrown it at him. His lips moved as if he were about to say something, and then he fell forward onto the floor.

Ruth raised her hands up to her mouth, then she gazed across at Jimmy.

"Jimmy!' she screamed, and then she ran across the chamber to him, knelt down in front of him and threw her arms around him.

"Oh Jimmy! Jimmy!" she cried. "Are you all right?"

She leaned back to look at his cut hands and face with tears running down her face.

"Help Ellie," Jimmy said, looking past her to Ellie who was still bound sobbing to the rack. "Help her," he said.

*

The king gasped loudly as his protective yellow light acting as a shield was broken. He now lay on the floor staring up at his brother, waiting for his brother's powerful red light to finish him off. Suddenly, Erin looked up and saw a brilliant white light now surrounding Rebecca. Erin stared at her in amazement as Rebecca, bathed in the white light's brilliance, looked as if she were an angel. Erin stopped what he was doing with the red light and moved away from his brother towards her.

An evil grin came onto his face as he raised his hand towards Rebecca, who remained still, kneeling and praying within the white light.

"I've always wanted to kill an angel," he said softly, as if speaking to himself.

The next moment, the brilliant light which surrounded Rebecca began to move across the chamber towards him. He gazed at it, his mouth opening in surprise, and then he stepped back, his red eyes now squinting in the light as it neared him. He raised his arms, trying to block out the light, trying to protect his eyes, and then he staggered back as the light engulfed him.

"No! No! Nooooo!!" he cried. "Aaaaaargh!!"

The king watched in horror as Erin now began to shrink back down to his original size and his skin started to crack. Suddenly, there was a loud noise as Erin's body seemed to explode, and then a huge cloud of dark dust rose up from where he had been standing. After a few moments, the light disappeared and the dust fell back down onto the floor. The next moment, they heard a sound like metal hitting the floor and saw the key which had been hanging around Erin's neck lying next to the settled dust. Slowly, the king raised himself back up onto his feet, staring first at the pile of dust that was once his brother, and then at the shining gold key that lay on the floor beside it.

CHAPTER 40

Rebecca stood beside the King in the darkened room as he knelt down in front of the large black box. He gazed at it for a moment holding the key in his hand, then he moved forward, placed the key into the lock and turned it. They heard a 'click'. At first, nothing happened. The King glanced up at Rebecca with a question in his expression, then suddenly, the darkness in the room began to disappear, shadows seemed to flee across the walls, the floor, and the ceiling, as light appeared, bathing the room and them both in its brightness. Rebecca turned to the window which had previously looked out upon the darkened sky and the non-stop storm. The dark clouds were disappearing and were replaced with a bright blue sky as the sun came out from behind the clouds and shone down upon the landscape below. Rebecca stared down at the surrounding fields, the forest, and the now calm ocean which sparkled beneath of the bright morning sun.

Where there was only the sound of the storm, birds could now be heard chirping and possibly singing as they flew from tree to tree. Flowers which had previously seemed dull now shone colourfully, reaching up to the sun-filled sky as if with renewed strength. The king stood up and gazed out of the window behind Rebecca. When Rebecca turned to smile at him, he grasped her hands, and with tears in his eyes, he smiled gratefully back at her.

"Thank you!" he said, with a deep emotion in his voice. "Thank you!"

*

Jimmy limped across the field. His face, hands and right arm were injured, as well as his left leg.

Rebecca, who was walking beside him, gave him a concerned look.

"Are you all right?" she asked.

She moved closer to him to take his arm. "Here, let me help you."

"I'll be okay," he said, continuing to limp on by himself.

"He said he prefers to be left alone," Ruth said, looking at Jimmy sadly from behind.

Rebecca looked back at Ruth who was holding Ellie's hand and leading her across the field.

"How is she?" Rebecca asked.

"Still the same," Ruth said, glancing at Ellie, who was walking beside Ruth with glazed staring eyes. "I think she's in a state of shock."

Rebecca looked back at Jimmy and observed the way he was limping.

"Do you want to rest?" she asked.

Jimmy glanced at her, "I want to go back," he said. "Who knows if the gate will disappear? I don't want to be stuck here."

The King, who was walking nearby with both Sev and Roe at his side, looked across at him, "And if you were stuck here," he said. "Would it be so bad? Now the Darkness has gone, this is a beautiful world. And more than that, you are heroes! All of you!"

Jimmy regarded the place where the large triangular gateway had once stood and had now disappeared, "I appreciate the offer." he said, "But it's not my world, it's not ... 'our' world. If I stayed, I would feel ... I would feel ..."

"Too tall?" the King suggested, raising his eyebrows with a smile towards Jimmy.

Jimmy shook his head, "No, it's ... it's not just that."

He glanced back at both Ruth and Ellie and the King noticed the look in his eyes.

"Ah! Love!" the King said, his smile widening.

Jimmy gave him a look and continued to limp on.

They reached the swirling gateway through which they had entered the small people's world. It spun like a mini cyclone in the field in exactly the same place as Rebecca and Jimmy had left it the last time they returned, but this time, instead of being black, it was now colourful.

"It's ... it's beautiful!" Rebecca said, staring at it as they stopped just a few yards from where it spun.

"Are you sure you won't stay?" the King asked.

Rebecca looked at him and returned his smile, "You have a beautiful world," she said. "It's hard to say no, but ... our world, our home, is somewhere else."

The King nodded, "I understand," he said.

Both Sev and Roe stepped forward to hug both Rebecca and Jimmy, and also Ruth.

"Take care of your friend," Sev said to Ruth as she glanced at Ellie.

"I will," Ruth said, returning Sev's smile.

Both Sev and Roe turned and went back to stand beside the King.

"We will never forget you!" Roe said, raising his hand to wave goodbye.

'We will never forget you!" Rebecca said, smiling at him.

Rebecca glanced at both Jimmy and Ruth, "Are you ready?" she asked.

"Ready," Jimmy said.

Ruth nodded, grasping Ellie's hand tightly in hers.

"Goodbye," the King said.

Rebecca looked at him, and then at Sev and Roe one last time.

"Goodbye," she said, and then she turned and leapt forward beneath the swirling and now colourful gateway, followed by Jimmy and Ruth, who leapt forward pulling Ellie behind her.

*

Back in the castle, in the dimly lit torture chamber, Krawl opened his eyes. He sat up and felt the pain from the knife still imbedded in his chest. He gasped, staring down at it, and then grunted as he brought his hands forward, gripped the knife's handle, and then, with a cry of pain, pulled it out. He dropped the knife and heard it clatter to the floor beside him. Placing a hand on his chest to cover the wound, he looked around to see that he was still in the torture chamber and that Ellie had gone. Suddenly, without warning, the torture chamber began to shake. Krawl glanced around, his eyes widening, wondering what was happening. A noise sounded to his right, and then a dark spiraling circular shape appeared from nowhere. Krawl stared at it, and then saw an image begin to form within the dark circle. The darkness disappeared and was suddenly replaced by an image of another world, a beautiful world with a clear blue sky above fields of grass, colourful flowers and rolling hills. He stared at the scene in front of him in wide-eyed silence, and then a voice spoke. It was deep, inhuman, it was a voice he had heard once before, and it sent a cold shiver down his spine.

"YOU ... WILL ... COME ... INTO ... MY ... WORLD!"

And then, without warning, a dark shadow seemed to emerge from the image in front of him. At first, it remained still, and then slowly, the dark shadow extended towards him, encircling him, and pulled him back towards the swirling circular gateway.

Krawl cried out loudly as he was pulled from the torture chamber and into the gateway to enter the other world. As he was pulled inside, the ground he now gazed down upon had turned red. Gone was the blue sky, the grass, the flowers, and the rolling hills, instead, they were replaced by a blood red nightmarish landscape of indescribable horror. As Krawl now knelt on the blood red ground, a gigantic figure appeared before him. It was wearing a black cloak with a hood, but he could still see the hideous face and the two large horns rising from its head.

"WECOME BACK TO MY WORLD!" it said, staring down at him with large red piercing eyes, and a deeply menacing grin which showed its sharp pointed teeth.

Krawl screamed loudly.

CHAPTER 41

Jimmy walked slowly along the street, the lapels of his coat pulled up high to hide the scars on his face from passers-by.

"Jimmy!" the voice called out to him from across the street.

Jimmy turned to see Rebecca running across the road to join him.

"I knew you'd come!" she said. "I'm so pleased to see you Jimmy!"

Jimmy kept his head lowered as he spoke.

"I ... I promised," he said. "But ... I can't stay!"

Rebecca touched his arm gently.

"Jimmy ... I want to help you. Please, come in! The people are kind, they ... they will help you find a home! 'I' will help you find a home! Please Jimmy! Come inside!"

Rebecca pulled Jimmy across the street towards the church. Jimmy stopped walking as they reached the church steps.

"Rebecca … I … I'm okay," he said with a shrug. "Really!"

Rebecca looked at him. Jimmy could see the concern in her eyes.

"But … you're living on the street again!" Rebecca said.

Jimmy gave another shrug, "Maybe that's where I belong," he said.

Rebecca shook her head.

"No, Jimmy! You don't! Please! I … I'm your friend! You know that, right?"

Jimmy hesitated, lowering his head again, then nodded.

He glanced across the street and saw Ellie and Ruth come out of a shop.

"Has … has Ellie remembered anything yet?" Jimmy asked.

Rebecca glanced across the street towards her two friends., then shook her head, "No, she doesn't remember anything. Nobody does apparently, except you, me and Ruth. It's like everyone's minds have been wiped blank. Everything's back to normal. The police are looking for missing persons, for them it's a mystery, all the bodies have disappeared."

Both Ellie and Ruth saw Rebecca and called out to her, then started walking across the road towards them.

"Maybe it's for the best that Ellie can't remember," Jimmy said.

"Jimmy," Rebecca said, gazing into his eyes and squeezing his arm tenderly, "I know that you got those scars saving Ellie. I know that you almost died to save her."

"But she doesn't know that," Jimmy said.

"Jimmy ... let me tell her, try to explain to her."

Jimmy shook his head, "I don't want her to remember," he said. "I don't want her to suffer ... like she did before."

Rebecca glanced at her friends who were walking towards them.

"And Ruth?" she said. "You know she feels something for you."

Jimmy shook his head, "I'm where I belong," he said. "I'm in my world."

He looked at her, and Rebecca was sure that she could see tears in his eyes.

"Take care," Jimmy said, then he turned and walked away.

"Jimmy!" Rebecca called after him.

There were tears in Rebecca's eyes as she watched him walk away back along the street.

Both Ellie and Ruth reached her.

"What are you talking to that bum for?" Ellie asked, glancing towards Jimmy as he walked away. "He's just a nobody! Have you seen those scars on his face? Eeeurk!!"

Ruth remained silent, staring along the street towards Jimmy as he walked away.

"Hey!" Ellie said, studying Rebecca curiously. "I know you've got a good heart and all that, but why do you want to help him? He's just a tramp! You're just wasting your time helping people like that!"

Rebecca looked at her. She was about to say something, then thought better of it.

"I ... I have to go," she said.

"Where are you going?" Ellie asked.

"I'm going to church," Rebecca said.

"To church?" Ellie repeated in a surprised voice. "Aren't you coming with us? We're going shopping for clothes!"

Rebecca looked at her for a moment, then glanced at Ruth, "He ... he needs someone," she said.

Ruth glanced once again along the street towards Jimmy who was walking away, "But ... I don't think ..." she started to say.

"Try," Rebecca said, looking at her.

Ellie glanced at them both, "What the hell are you two talking about?" she asked.

Rebecca glanced at her, then turned and went up the steps towards the church.

"When did she become religious?" Ellie asked. "Well, it doesn't matter." She turned to Ruth, "Let's go shopping!" she said.

Ruth continued to look along the street towards Jimmy, "I ... I ..."

She glanced back at Ellie, "Sorry," she said. "I have to go!"

Ellie stood, her mouth gaping open in surprise, as she watched Ruth begin to run along the street.

"What the hell ...!" Ellie said to herself, watching her go.

*

Jimmy turned as he heard his name being called and saw Ruth who had now stopped running and was standing behind him.

"Jimmy," Ruth said.

Jimmy looked back at her, pulling the lapels of his coat further up to hide the scars on his face.

Ruth held out her hand towards him.

"Jimmy, take my hand," she said softly.

Jimmy continued to look at her, then he shook his head.

"We ... we're not in that place anymore," he said.

"I don't care," Ruth said. "Please, Jimmy, take my hand."

"But ... but you're safe now! You ... you don't need to hold my hand anymore."

"Please? ... Jimmy?"

Jimmy lowered his head, "I ... I have scars," he said. "And you ... you belong in another world."

Ruth approached him.

She reached out and lifted his face to gaze into his eyes and saw his tears.

"We are in the same world," she said softly. Then she took his hand and grasped it tightly in hers.

"Jimmy," she whispered, saying his name softly with a smile, still gazing into his eyes.

Then she leaned forward and kissed him on his lips,

*

In another part of the city, a small man came staggering out of the large red building opposite the park and stood looking around with one hand to his head.

He felt dizzy and his head hurt him, in fact, he wasn't feeling good at all.

Suddenly, he saw a car pass by on the road in front of him. The small man raised his eyebrows staring at the passing car in amazement.

"Where the hell am I?" Tol said to himself.

The End

ABOUT THE AUTHOR

Lawrence Nabbs (Larry) was born in London, England. He wrote his first short story at the age of eleven. He later started to write poems and other short stories. He was given the idea for his first novel length story after having had the strange experience of seeing UFOs in France. Since then, Larry has enjoyed writing novel length stories, but still writes poems from time to time. In England, he did different jobs, not really finding himself until he went to Paris, France, to become an English teacher where he lived and worked as a teacher for over twenty years, therefore he also speaks French. He later went to Beijing, China, in the year 2006 where he continues to teach English and write novel length stories, such as crime thrillers, science fiction and fantasies. He has also written stories for a children's comic in China for learning English. He loves the cinema, films of all kinds, as well as books and music. He likes and very often writes stories in cafes, and also loves the feeling of being near the ocean.